PIECING HIS
LOVE

PIECING HIS
LOVE

MARY ROZA

BALBOA.
PRESS

A DIVISION OF HAY HOUSE

Balboa Press books may be ordered through booksellers or by contacting:

Balboa Press
A Division of Hay House
1663 Liberty Drive
Bloomington, IN 47403
www.balboapress.com
1-(877) 407-4847

ISBN: 978-1-4525-4165-5 (e)
ISBN: 978-1-4525-4164-8 (sc)

Library of Congress Control Number: 2011919624

Printed in the United States of America

Balboa Press rev. date: 02/16/2012

CHAPTER ONE

The Beginning of Love

William Valmont wasn't always a good guy. He used to be a troubled kid with a bad past, until he met Mary Radcliffe. They first met at Shales Elementary School. William, thirteen years old and was held back in elementary school for two years. Mary, ten years old and she past all her school grades. It was a Thursday afternoon right after lunch when it all happened. It was recess and Mary was with two of her friends, Ash Donnellson and Misty Lombard playing basketball when Mary's other friend, Allison Jackson ran up to her in tears.

"Allison, what's wrong? What happened?" Mary hugged Allison.

"Mary, for the last three days, this boy started teasing me and he won't leave me alone!" Allison cried.

"Where is this boy, I would like to talk to him. Where is he?" Mary, angrily at the boy who teased her friend.

"His name is William Valmont. He's a sixth grader and he's over by the monkey bars!"

"Hey Mare, what's with Allison?" Ash walked over to Mary, holding onto the basketball.

"I have to take care of a boy who's been teasing my friend. Tell Misty to hang on with the game Ash. I'll be right back. Come on Ally, let's go find him!" Mary walked with Allison to the monkey bars.

On the other side of the playground by the monkey bars, William Valmont sat on top of the bars when Allison came over with a girl with chocolate-brown hair.

"Well look who's come back for more teasing and look, you bought a friend as well!" William, evilly and jumped off the monkey bars.

"Look William, you leave my best friend alone otherwise I will report you!" Mary told William to stay away from Allison.

"Yeah right, like I'm going to listen to a couple of fifth graders, but I will give you a warning. You two better watch your backs, because I will stalk you and tease you throughout the rest of the year!" William gave Allison and Mary his warning and walked off.

"I wouldn't count on that!" Mary, not believing him.

From that day on, Mary and William became enemies. Everyday, William found Mary and Allison and bullied them until one Tuesday in October during recess. Ash waited for Mary by the swing set when he noticed Mary running towards him.

"Hey, what's going on Mary?" Ash asked as Mary hid behind him.

"Its William Valmont! He's coming for me!" Mary with fright.

"What!" Ash with a little anger.

"Okay. Where is she? I know that Mary is hiding behind you!" William went behind Ash.

"You leave Mary alone!" Ash grabbed Mary's hand and continued to hide her.

"Don't get into this boy; this is between Mary and I!" William pushed Ash back.

"Don't push me boy! Just leave Mary alone!" Ash defended Mary.

"Try and stop me defender of the coward." William called Mary a coward.

"Don't you dare call Mary a coward, creep!" Ash lunged himself at William.

The two started to fight as Mary tried to stop them, but Will accidentally slammed Mary into the ground.

"Get off of her! Get out of here before I report you!" Ash yelled as William ran off.

Ash helped Mary up and hugged her.

"Mare, are you okay?" Ash held her.

"Yeah, I'm fine. Thanks for coming to my rescue." Mary thanked her hero.

"No problem. Don't worry Mare, I won't let that William hurt you again. I promise, I will protect you no matter what happens." Ash touched Mary's hair.

Ever since that day, Ash protected Mary from the taunting and bulling from William. The hatred lasted all the way into January, the day that would change everything.

It was just a normal Monday at school during recess. Mary was miserable that Allison moved in late November to Iowa. Ash wasn't in class that day and all of Mary's friends played on the snow mountains.

Mary walked around the gymnasium building when she noticed William standing there. William noticed Mary and they stared at each other for a few minutes.

William noticed a long icicle hanging on the gymnasium wall. Before Mary turned around, the icicle broke off from the building.

"Mary, watch out! That icicle is going to hit you!" William warned Mary and he ran up to her.

Mary looked up at a huge icicle that fell right at her. William ran up to Mary and pushed her out of the target zone and the icicle hit his cheek. William fell to the ground with pain all over his face. He screamed and Mary ran to get help. She didn't understand why William rescued her from the icicle after he bullied her ever since September, but she had to help him.

After school, Mary saw William at the playground on the monkey bars. She felt concerned about him after the incident at lunch.

"Hey." Mary climbed onto the monkey bars and sat next to William.

"Hey." William answered Mary.

"How's your face?" Mary touched Will's face.

"It's okay. It still hurts though. I don't know how to explain this to my parents when I get home." William with sadness.

"Why did you save my life from that icicle even though we hate each other?"

"Mary, I saved your life, because I wanted to be your friend. I don't want us to be enemies for the rest of the school year. The reason why I picked on you and Allison is that I'm new to this school and if I was mean and tough, I could've made friends."

"You know, being tough and mean doesn't mean that you can make friends. If you just be yourself and let your goodness out, then you will have friends." Mary gave William advice.

"That's the thing Mary, I don't know how to be nice. I can't talk to any of my parents, because I came from a troubled family. I hardly have any friends and I really need a friend right now to help me through my troubled times." William sadly.

"I'll be your friend, William. Let's just forget about us being enemies and start fresh as friends." Mary hugged William.

"Thanks Mary. You are a really great friend. Come on, I'll walk you home." William smiled at Mary and climbed off the monkey bars.

"Your welcome Will. I'll be here for you no matter what happens." Mary promised as Will helped her climb down the monkey bars.

The months passed and before long it was May. It was the last day of school and everyone said goodbye to their friends for another summer.

"I can't believe that you are leaving and you won't come back next year." Mary, sadly to William.

The two friends were at the swings during recess talking about the summer ahead of them.

"I know. I can't believe I'm going to junior high at the end of the summer. Don't worry Mary, I'll see you over the summer and come over to your house." William promised Mary that they will keep in contact with each other.

"It just wouldn't be the same without you here next year." Mary said as Will pushed her on the swing.

"You'll see me after when you get out of Shales and go to Leavenston junior high if you go there for seventh grade." William pushed Mary.

"I hope I will go to Leavenston and see you." Mary hoped and looked at her friend.

What Mary didn't know was that William developed a secret crush on her.

2001 went by, Mary graduated elementary school and going onto junior high school.

It was Monday, August twenty-fourth, 2002 and it was Mary's first day at Leavenston junior high school.

In sixth grade, Mary made new friends and they were attending the same school as she was. Over the summer, Mary had to say goodbye to Ash and Misty since they were both attending Kanto junior high school instead of Leavenston. It was that same day that she would bump into an old friend.

It was right after fifth period when Mary headed to lunch with her friends Natalie Bakerton and Kaylin Robertson when she bumped into a guy.

"Oh my gosh, I'm so sorry for bumping into you." Mary apologized to the guy with glasses.

"That's okay. Everyone bumps into each other now and then. Oh, hey Mary." The boy looked up at the girl who bumped into him.

"Do I know you?" Mary, with a strange look on her face.

"Mary, it's me, William Valmont. Remember, the guy who teased you when I was in sixth grade and you were in fifth grade at Shales elementary school." William tried to let Mary remember him as he helped her up.

"Oh my god! Hi Will. I couldn't remember you with glasses on. I can't believe that you have glasses! When did you get them?" Mary remembered William.

"Last year during seventh grade, I got glasses, because I wasn't seeing too well with my normal vision. It's so good to finally see you again. I thought you'd never graduate elementary school." William, happily as he hugged Mary.

"I know. My sixth year went by slowly. I missed you too much last year. It wasn't the same at Shales without you. You look incredible with glasses. They make you look older and handsome." Mary complimented Will with his glasses.

"Thanks." William blushed.

"Mare, we'll meet you in the cafeteria. It was nice meeting you William." Natalie said to Mary as she and Kaylin walked away.

"Was that the guy Mary was talking about last year Natalie?"

"Yes. I'll tell you more about him when we get to lunch."

"So um, what class are you going to next Mary?"

"I'm going to lunch. Where are you going?"

"I'm going to lunch too. Here, I'll show you where the cafeteria is at." William guided Mary to the cafeteria.

At the cafeteria during sixth period, Mary and William spent the whole lunch hour talking about their sixth and seventh years of school.

Friday, December tenth, William noticed a poster for the Christmas dance that was next weekend.

"That's it, I'll ask Mary to the Christmas dance and then during the dance, I'll ask her out as my girlfriend. Oh, I hope she'll go to the Christmas dance with me and be my girl at the end of the night."

Later on, William couldn't wait to go to lunch and ask Mary to the dance. Time seemed slow for him and he wanted to see Mary again.

It was noon when the bell rang signaled the end of fifth period and passing period for sixth. Will met Mary at her locker and walked her to lunch.

"Okay, I have to make this work for next Saturday. I have to ask Mary to the dance whether I mess this up or not." William looked at Mary as they sat down at the lunch table.

After eating lunch, William decided to talk to Mary about the Christmas dance.

"Um, Mary, can I ask you something?" William, with a shaken tone.

"Yes, what is it?" Mary, with concern.

"You know that the Christmas dance is next Saturday, right?" William told Mary about the dance.

"Yeah, I know that the dance is next Saturday. Why do you ask?"

"Do you want to go to the dance with me next Saturday?"

"Yes, I would like to go to the dance with you!" Mary gleamed.

Will, relieved and happy that Mary accepted his request to go to the dance with him.

"Great. What time do you want me to come over to your house to pick you up?" William blushed.

"Around six." Mary answered.

"All right six it is." William smiled.

All William needed to do was to ask Mary out during the dance and hoped that she would be his girlfriend by the end of the night that Saturday.

Saturday, December eighteenth, 2002 was the night of the Christmas dance.

It was around six o'clock when William walked over to Mary's house to pick her up for the dance. The weather wasn't as chilly that evening, but the ground was covered with snow.

William was dressed in a navy blue dress shirt and black pants with black shoes. He rang the doorbell and Mary's mother, Petra Radcliffe answered the door.

"Hello Mrs. Radcliffe, is Mary there? I'm here to pick her up for the dance." William he greeted himself.

"Yes she is William. Come on in, I'll go get her for you. It's great to see you again William. How've you been?" Petra let William in and both walked into the living room.

"I've been okay. School's going great for me."

"That's good. Let me go get Mary. I'll and tell her that you are here. Make yourself at home while I go get her." Petra went upstairs.

A few minutes went by and Mary came downstairs with her mom as William talked to Mary's father, Andrew about school. Mary was in a dark purple short dress with silver shoes. Her hair was straightened and half-curled.

"Wow Mary, you look amazing tonight." William looked at Mary.

"You look handsome yourself tonight Will." Mary, with surprise as she looked at William.

In his mind, William knew that he took the most beautiful girl to the Christmas dance and he looked at Mary with amazement.

At the Leavenston gymnasium, the room decorated with Christmas decorations with dim lights, snowflakes, and a Christmas tree in the middle of the room.

Once the dance music came on, William plucked up courage to ask Mary for a dance.

"Mary, would you like to dance with me?"

"Yeah, sure." Mary got up from her seat.

William led Mary to the dance floor with his hand in hers.

"You know, I am so glad that I asked you to go to the dance with me tonight." William held Mary as they danced.

"I'm glad that you asked me to the dance. You are such a gentleman and I'm having a wonderful time with you tonight." Mary looked into William's eyes.

"Mary, I need to tell you something." Will looked at Mary.

"What is it?" Mary with a puzzled look.

"Remember, when we were in elementary school and when we first became friends?" Will asked Mary if she remembered when they first met.

"Yes I remember. Why do you ask?" Mary, with concern.

"Well after we became friends, I started to have a crush on you. After I left Shales, I missed you and thought about you everyday. I wanted to tell you my feelings for you, but I couldn't tell you until now. Mary, I like you a lot and will you be my girlfriend?" William told Mary how much he felt about her.

"Yes, I will be your girlfriend, William." Mary accepted Will's request.

"Mary, you just made this night, the best night of my life!" William hugged Mary tightly in his arms.

"I know and I'm glad that you are my boyfriend, my only boyfriend." Mary held onto William.

"I had a wonderful night with you, Will." Mary walked up to the front porch.

"I know you did. I had fun with you too." William smiled.

"Here, it's my number. Call me tomorrow and I'll see you in school on Monday." Mary looked inside her purse for her keys.

"I will."

"See you." Mary hugged Will.

As William walked off Mary's porch, he realized that he forgot to give something to Mary.

"Mary wait!" William ran back onto the porch and stopped Mary before she walked into the house.

"What is it?" Mary asked suddenly.

William took a breath, stared at Mary for a couple of seconds, and kissed her on the lips. After a couple of seconds later, they broke apart.

"Wow that was a brilliant kiss." Mary, dazed.

"I know, for our first kiss." William glowed red in the face.

"My first kiss with you." Mary smiled and blushed.

For the rest of the school year, Mary and William remained together. Everyone at Leavenston knew that William and Mary would be together and that they were meant for each other.

In 2003, William graduated from Leavenston and moved onto Lake Park high school. Mary stayed at Leavenston for her eighth grade year. William walked Mary home after school and saw her everyday.

It looked like the year was going perfectly for them until a couple of days after Christmas vacation started. It was a Sunday and Mary spent the day with William when it all started.

"Will, what's this? Are these suspension notices and detention slips?" Mary looked on her boyfriend's desktop.

"Huh? Oh, yes they are." William looked up from his Algebra textbook.

"Why do you have these slips? Are you getting yourself into trouble at school? Please William, tell me what's going on?" Mary asked for the truth.

"Okay Mary, here's the truth. Lately, ever since my family has told me not to join the basketball team, I decided to enact with revenge on my parents by getting into trouble, skipping class, and not doing my homework, but they never noticed since they don't care about me anyways. You are the first person to notice my troublemaking self."

"William, you have to stop making trouble. You won't be able to pass freshman year and keep up with your class if you keep on causing trouble. Please, I want you to succeed, not cause trouble." Mary begged.

"I really want to, but my parents won't notice my troubles. God, I just wish that they would notice already!" William angrily shoved his Algebra book off his bed.

"Don't worry, I'll find a way to make your parents notice." Mary put her arms around her boyfriend's shoulders to comfort him.

During dinner, Petra noticed her daughter's change.

"Mary, is there anything you would like to discuss with us?" Petra with concern.

"Today, when I was at William's house, I noticed that he had detention slips and a suspension notice from his school. I asked him why he was getting into trouble and he told me that he wanted to get his parent's attention since they didn't let him play on the freshman basketball team this year and they don't care about him." Mary told her parents the story.

"I think that is awful for parents not to raise their kids with the proper care and love that they need in this life!" Andrew, with anger.

"I was thinking that maybe we should invite William and his parents here to our house for Christmas dinner and reunite their shattered family." Mary spilled out her idea to her mom and dad.

"I think that is a very good idea Mary. We should do that and everything will be back to normal and William can move on in his high school career." Petra agreed with her daughter.

"Okay dear. Mary, you better call William and invite him to our house for Christmas." Andrew told Mary.

Mary got up from the dining room table and walked into the kitchen. She picked up the phone and called her boyfriend.

"William, the plan is on. I just talked to my parents about your troubles and they agreed to help you. I want you to come with your parents on Christmas to have dinner with us." Mary told the plans to her boyfriend.

"Okay. I hope this plan will work Mary." William hoped.

"Don't worry, this plan will work. Trust me." Mary brought faith to her boyfriend.

Sunday, December twenty-fifth, 2003 was Christmas.

Around six that evening, William and his parents, Ryan and Claire came over to meet Mary's parents and have dinner.

During dinner, Mary noticed Ryan only putting small portions on his son's plate. Andrew took notice after he saw his daughter's reaction on her face.

"Here Ryan, let me fill William's plate." Andrew he got up and took the plate from Ryan.

"Oh thank you Andrew." Ryan, with relief and continued to eat.
Later on,

"Mom, could you pass the potatoes please?"

Claire didn't notice her son's question.

"I'll get the potatoes for you Will." Petra passed the bowl.

"Thank you Mrs. Radcliffe." William scooped some potatoes on his plate.

"Mr. and Mrs. Valmont, I think your son is a wonderful guy with a lot of ambition, but you need to help him become a better person instead of always bringing him down and critizing him."

Ryan and Claire looked at each other, then Mary, and then at their son who was in the living room.

"The reason why he is getting into trouble is that he wants your attention, because he wants you to love him instead of hating him. You need to be better parents and love your son more. He needs you right now during his high school years and the rest of his life for guidance. Please, just listen to me and just love your son just like every parent does." Mary told William's parents to love him, got up from the dining room table, and walked over to William in the living room.

"You know what Ryan, Mary is right. We've been terrible parents to William since he was in fifth grade and he needs our help more than ever during his high school years." Claire told her husband.

"You're right Claire. We should reconcile with our son and give him our love and respect. We were bad parents to William." Ryan with guilt.

"What you need to do is to apologize to William and tell him how much you love and care about him." Andrew looked in the living room to see his daughter cheering up William.

You are right Andrew. We need to bring our family back together again and be good parents to William." Claire got up from the table, walked over to the living room, hugged her son, and cried.

"You are very lucky to have a daughter like Mary, looking out for our son and protecting him." Ryan proudly to Andrew and complimented his daughter.

"I know and she's lucky to have your son in her life." Andrew watched Ryan got up from the table, walked up to William, and hugged him.

"William, we are very sorry for treating you like dirt and not loving you as our son." Claire sobbed and held onto her son.

"We promise to always be there for you and treat you better as good parents should be." Ryan apologized to his son and held him.

"Thanks mom, dad. I promise to stay out of trouble and become a hard worker again. I forgive you, my parents." William, happily held onto his parents.

"Thank you Mary, Andrew, and Petra. You made us realize that we needed to bring our troubled family back together and bring back the love to our family." Ryan thanked Mary's family.

"If you need help anytime, we will be there to help you out. Our friends."

"Then you are a part of our family."

Later on that evening, Mary and William were outside on the back porch looking at the stars.

"Mary, thank you for bringing my family back together again. It feels like I'm whole again!" William hugged his girl.

"Hey, I'd do anything for you. No matter what happens to us." Mary looked into her boyfriend's eyes for a few minutes and kissed him.

The two kissed for a long time and started to make out for the first time underneath the stars and the frosty full moon.

CHAPTER TWO

Breaking Up and Making Up

In 2004, Mary graduated Leavenston and moved onto Lake Park high school. Mary was happy to see all her old friends and her boyfriend again including Kaylin Robertson, Jessie Sootburg, Susan Kittle, and Natalie Bakerton. Mary had few classes with her friends, but she only had one class with William.

By the time sophomore and junior year arrived for Mary and William, he fell out of love with her.

This all happened at Langston park one afternoon on Saturday, May twenty-seventh, 2005. William played basketball with his friends, James Pickett, Ron Handleton, and Alex Hudson.

"Well, there goes the ball." James yelled as the ball rolled off the court.

"Don't worry, I'll get it." William ran off the court and into the trees.

William found the ball next to a girl who sat on the bench.

"Hey, could you hand me the ball that's next to the bench?"

"Sure. Oh man, you're William Valmont, the star athlete in school! I'm Felicia Millerton." Felicia introduced herself to William and blushed.

"Nice to meet you Felicia. I never seen you at school before."

"Yeah, I came to Lake Park high in 2005. I always go to the basketball and football games and I cheer for you."

"Really, thanks. Yeah, I am a great football player and I do my best out on the field. Hey, you want to watch me play basketball with a couple of my friends?"

"Sure. I'd like that." Felicia smiled.

Throughout the whole game, Felicia cheered William as he beat Ron in the end with thirty points.

"Wow Will, you were amazing out there! I can't believe that you beat your friend thirty points to ten points." Felicia, with amazement.

"Well, he shouldn't have challenged me since he is so bad at basketball." William felt happy for himself.

"You know, I had a lot of fun with you Will. I'm so glad I could finally meet you. Ever since I was a freshman and I saw you at the first game, I've been having a crush on you." Felicia spilled out her feelings for William.

"Really?"

"Yeah." Felicia drew closer to William and kissed him straight on the lips.

After kissing for two minutes, they broke apart.

"Here Will, this is my cell number. Call me sometime okay. I'll see you in school sometime." Felicia glowed red, gave Will a folded piece of paper, and walked away.

William glowed red in the face as he watched Felicia walk away. He fell for Felicia as he looked at her number. Will wanted to ask her out, but he was going out with Mary.

"If I really want to go out with Felicia, I need to break up with Mary. I guess we do need to take a break for a while since I became distant with her. I have to go where my heart decides and I want Felicia as my girlfriend."

Saturday, June fourteenth, 2006, Mary was at the mall with Natalie and Stephanie Berenson. They were at the fountain resting for a couple of minutes when Mary's cell phone vibrated. She checked out the caller ID on her phone and it was William.

"Hey babe, what's up?" Mary happily into the phone.

"Mary, we need to talk about us and our relationship." William, with a serious tone.

"What about our relationship?" Mary, with concern.

"I'm sorry to do this, but I'm breaking up with you." William, coldly to Mary.

"Why? Why do you want to break up with me? Did I do something wrong?" Mary panicked.

"No, you didn't do anything wrong. Its just that we've been growing apart ever since the end of last year. I am starting to like this girl named Felicia Millerton. I really want to ask her out, but I need to end it with you first. I'm sorry for breaking your heart Mary, but I really want to be your friend for now."

"You know what, you are right. We've been separating for the last few months ever since I started my writing career. Go be with Felicia if that's what you want. We can still be friends if you want to. Listen, I gotta go." Mary, sadly.

"I'm really sorry to do this to you Mare. I'll check on you tomorrow when I come over. I'll talk to you later. Bye."

Mary hung up on William before he said goodbye to her. Soon after, she broke down into tears.

Natalie, noticed Mary crying, went up to her with concern.

"Mary, are you all right? Tell me what's going on?" Natalie sat next to her friend.

"No! William dumped me for another girl!" Mary sobbed onto Natalie's shoulder.

"Oh Mary, I'm sorry. I always thought that you two would last forever." Natalie hugged her friend and tried to cheer her up.

"It's all my fault. If I only paid more attention to him, I wouldn't have lost him." Mary with guilt through her tears.

Throughout the summer, William and Mary remained friends while he dated Felicia. They hardly talked to each other since Felicia hated Mary and she wanted her boyfriend to stay away from her. By the time school started, Mary started to miss William.

"Come on Mare, it's the first game of the season. You have to go!" Eric, tried to convince her to go to the football game.

It was a Friday afternoon after school, Mary was at Kaylin's house with Eric. Kaylin, Tyler, and Kevin before heading to the football game at the school.

"I can't Eric. I got a lot of homework to do tonight." Mary made an excuse.

"Mare, it's the first few days of school. We don't get any homework. What's the matter? Why don't you want to go to the game with us?"

"I bet you its William. You miss him. Do you Mary?" Kevin took a guess.

"Kevin's right. I do miss Will. The reason why I don't want to go to the game is that Felicia will be there and she won't let William talk to me. It feels like she hypnotized him and ruined our relationship." Mary told the truth to her friends.

"Mary, William broke your heart. He'll always remember that and he'll regret it. He will if something goes wrong in his relationship with Felicia. You'll see." Kaylin advised Mary.

"You're right Kaylin. You know, I'm going to write my Star Sisters story tonight. I'll see you guys tomorrow." Mary walked home.

By the time homecoming came, Mary didn't attend any of the events or even the dance. William got concerned about Mary.

"Natalie, is Mary here? I need to talk to her."

"I'm sorry Will, but Mary didn't show up to the dance all because of you and your girlfriend!" Natalie told the story to William.

"Oh man. I better call her and see how she's doing." William took out his phone and dialed Mary's number.

"I would do that Will." Natalie walked away.

"Hello?" Mary answered her cell phone.

"Mary, its William. How are you?"

"I've been lonely without you talking to me and being my friend. I miss you!" Mary, sadly to Will.

"I know, I know. Natalie told me the whole story. I miss too Mare. I'll come by tomorrow and we'll save our friendship. Felicia doesn't have to know about our friendship." William made a promise to Mary.

"Okay, that's fine with me." Mary, happily through the phone.

By the time May arrived, William and Mary's friendship grew closer and stronger, but Mary didn't go to his games, because of Felicia.

One Tuesday on the last day of April, Mary was at Langston Park with Stephanie.

"So Mary, are you going to prom this year?"

"Oh prom. Well... I... I'm not going this year."

"Why not?" Stephanie questioned Mary.

"Since last year, I promised that I wanted to go to prom only if William asked me, but since we broke up, I can't go."

"Oh yeah and William is taking Felicia to the prom. You know Mary, there is something that I need to tell you. A few weeks ago when I had my sleepover with Felicia. You know the one you couldn't make it to."

"Yeah I remember. What happened?" Mary, with curiosity.

"Well, she told me that the reason why she is going out with William was that so she can use him. She never had a crush on him and she never loved him. She's only playing with his heart ever since June. Felicia also told me that she's been hooking up with other guys and forgetting about William." Stephanie told Mary about Felicia's unfaithfulness.

"Oh my god, that little bitch! How dare she mess with my best friend and the one I still love his heart!" Mary, angrily as her fists grew together.

"Look, I know that you still love William and you don't want to see him get hurt, but he needs to know the truth first." Stephanie calmed her friend down.

"I can't let William get hurt! I have to tell him that his girlfriend is cheating on him!" Mary grabbed her cell phone and dialed William's number.

On the other side of the pond, Mary waited anxiously for Will to pick up his phone.

"Hello?" William picked up the phone.

"Hey Will, its Mary."

"Hey Mare, what's up?"

"William, I need to tell you something. It's about Felicia." Mary, sternly.

"What about Felicia? Is she all right?" William, with concern about his girlfriend.

"William, Felicia is cheating on you. I heard not too long ago that Felicia is just using you to get other guys and she doesn't love you. She lied to you about having a crush on you and she's just playing with your heart." Mary told William everything.

"No, no, no, I don't believe you Mary! Felicia would never cheat on me! You are just jealous of Felicia, because I chose her over you! You are lying to me! We can't be friends if you are lying to me." William, angrily to Mary.

"I'm not lying to you William. I'm telling you the truth!" Mary defended herself.

"You know what, just do me a favor and leave me alone! Go to hell Mary!" William with anger and hung up on Mary.

Mary, ashamed that William didn't believe that his girlfriend cheated on him and that she hypnotized him. Mary went back betrayed and embarrassed.

Friday, May seventeenth, 2007 was prom night. Stephanie and Natalie went over to Mary's house with their dates to check up on her before they went to prom.

"Come on Mare, come to prom with us!" Stephanie tried to convince Mary to come to the dance.

"I can't. I've got a lot of homework to do tonight and I don't even have a dress or anything."

"Hey, if you come in your nightgown, I'll give you fifty bucks." Joey advised Mary.

"Cut it out Joey! Mary, throughout the whole year, you never went to one school event. Next year, you are going to all of the events no matter what you say."

"All right, I'll go to prom next year. You guys go on ahead without me. Have fun tonight." Mary kept her promise.

"We will. Don't worry Mare, once William graduates we will have a lot of fun during our senior year." Stephanie hugged Mary.

At the Starlight hotel, everyone was having a great time. After dinner was served, the dancing began. William noticed all of Mary's friends were at prom, but Mary wasn't.

"Stephanie, where's Mary? I really need to talk to her."

"Well, she isn't here. She didn't want to come tonight all because of you. You know, Mary was telling you the truth about Felicia, but you didn't listen to her."

"Come on baby! Let's dance! I've got something to show you." Felicia dragged her boyfriend away from Stephanie.

Out on the dance floor, Felicia danced with her boyfriend and she pulled out something out of her purse.

"Babe, I want our night to be our special night together. Yesterday, I reserved a suite in this hotel to make our night special." Felicia showed William the key.

William didn't pay attention to his girlfriend, he thought about Mary and how guilty he felt by hurting her. He needed to see her and apologize to her.

"Look Felicia, I can't go to the room with you. I think I'll go home instead. I'll call you later." William turned down the offer with his girl and walked away.

"William wait!" Felicia tried to stop her boyfriend, but he already left the ballroom.

Felicia walked out of the ballroom, angry that William ditched her and that she wasn't going to give herself to him on prom night.

Josh Eaglewood, a senior classmate came out of the men's washroom and found Felicia on the floor in tears.

"Hey, why are you here all alone without a date?" Josh tried to cheer Felicia up.

"My stupid boyfriend decides to ditch me to go home! I hate him so much right now!" Felicia, angrily wiped her tears.

"I'm sorry. My date ditched me too for another guy." Josh, miserably.

"Really?" Felicia looked at Josh

"Yeah. Hey, do you want to be my prom date?" Josh stroked Felicia's hair.

"Sure, I like that." Felicia cheered up.

"Come on, let's dance." Josh took Felicia's hand and led her to the ballroom.

After a few dances, Josh and Felicia connected with each other as Mary's friends were shocked to see Felicia cheating on William.

"Hey, do you want to go to my hotel room?" Felicia showed him the key.

"Sure. Once we get up there, I will show you a night that you won't ever forget." Josh walked to the elevator and kissed her.

By the end of the night, Felicia gave herself to Josh behind William's back and hooked up with Josh.

Meanwhile, Mary finished up her Child Ed project when she heard the doorbell. She opened the door to find Will with a pink rose.

"William, what are you doing here? Aren't you suppost to be at prom with Felicia?" Mary, with surprise.

"Look, I came from prom, because I wasn't having fun without you there. I was thinking about you and I wanted to apologize to you. I am sorry for yelling at you and hanging up on you like that. I shouldn't have done that to you." William apologized and he gave her the rose.

"Oh William, I forgive you, but I was telling you the truth about Felicia." Mary looked at the rose.

"I know that you've been hearing bad things about Felicia, but she said to me that they were just rumors and that they weren't true. She's true to me and she loves me. It was just that people were putting shit on my girlfriend and I had to protect her."

"I know, I understand. The reason why I didn't go to prom was because of Felicia. If I went, she wouldn't let me talk to you or even dance with you." Mary looked at William.

"I know, but Felicia isn't here to stop me from dancing with you." William looked at Mary.

"Will, I'm not dressed. I'm not ready." Mary looked at her clothes with shame.

"It doesn't matter Mary. You look beautiful to me in your pink nightgown. Come on, I want to dance with you in the backyard." William took Mary's hand and led her to the backyard.

William took Mary's left hand and placed it around his neck and her right hand in his. They danced around the yard as lighting bugs glowed around them.

"Mare, are you having fun?"

"Yes, I am. You really made my night special Will. Thank you for coming by and dancing with me." Mary smiled and leaned against William.

"You're welcome. I'm just glad that we are talking again." William held Mary tightly and stroked her hair.

Two weeks past, William drifted away from Felicia and fell in love with Mary again. Felicia spent more time with Josh more than with William. On Saturday, May twenty-ninth, 2007 was the day of William's graduation.

"Mary, I'm glad that you came to my graduation! Now you know how it feels next year when you go get your diploma." William placed his cap on Mary's head and his arm around her.

"I know and I am so proud of you for walking across the stage and receiving your diploma. So, what are you going to do now that you are a high school graduate?" Mary hugged William and entered the hallway.

"I'm going to still stay in Lake Park and go to Lake Park Community College to study in Criminal Justice. I want to be a police detective just like my father." William told Mary his plans.

"That's wonderful Will. I hope that you will keep in contact with me when you go to college." Mary, happily for her friend.

"You bet I will Mare. You are a great friend to me!" William held onto Mary.

The next thing William and Mary knew was that Felicia came up to them with Josh.

"William, we need to talk about us. You know, ever since you ditched me at prom, we became separate and I did something to help me get through for what you did at prom. I hooked up with Josh Eaglewood on prom night and he just asked me to be his girlfriend. So, I decided to dump you for Josh and we're leaving town tonight." Felicia dumped William for Josh.

"You know what, fine! Go be with him! Just stay out of my life! It was a waste of time dating you!"

Felicia walked up to William, slapped him, and walked away from Josh while Mary saw the whole thing. William stood there for a couple of minutes and quickly walked out of the school. Mary followed him soon after.

"William wait up! Look, I'm sorry about what happened between you and Felicia just now." Mary walked out to the field.

"Don't say you're sorry Mary! You and Stephanie were right about Felicia. She loves to enjoy hurting people. This is all my fault! What was I thinking of dating Felicia!" William blamed himself and freaked out.

"It's not your fault Will. This had to happen. Felicia dumped you, because she is cruel. She's an evil person and you're a good person. Since the day you stayed out of trouble, you have been doing great things and I'm proud of you. You need someone that will love you for who you are and who won't betray you." Mary touched William's face as they sat on a rock.

"But I fear that I won't find that special someone. I'll be alone for the rest of my life."

"You will one day, but right now, I'll be here for you to take care of you and protect you. I will always be there for you if you need me." Mary promised to William.

William looked at Mary deep within her eyes and he knew that Mary was the one for him.

"Mary, there is something that I need to tell you. Mary, I'm still in love with you. Ever since prom night when I came over to your house, I started to like you again. You were the only person that I could count on in my life. You helped me through my troubled times over the years. I fell in love with you and even though we broke up last summer, I still loved you. I love you Mary and I never stopped loving you." William spilled out his love.

"Oh Will, there is something I have to tell you as well. I still have feelings for you too. Ever since you went out with Felicia, I thought I lost you forever. I was jealous of you and her together. Once I found out that Felicia cheated on you, I had to tell you, but you didn't believe me and I thought that you didn't love me anymore, but you still do. William, I still want to be with you and I want another chance with you. I love you. I always had." Mary held William's face and spilled her feelings.

William looked at Mary for a couple of minutes and kissed her on the lips.

"Wow, I missed that." Mary dazed after Will kissed her.

"I know you have. Mary, will you be my girlfriend again?" William held both of her hands.

"Yes William. I will be your girlfriend again and I promise that I will give you more attention and I'll be a better girlfriend to you than ever before." Mary promised William to be perfect to him.

"Mary, you were always the best girlfriend to me, because you changed my life and now I realize that I want you to be by my side for the rest of my life. I love you Mary and I don't want to lose you again." William held Mary as he promised to her that he'll love her and be there for her.

Mary nodded and smiled as William helped her off the rock.

"I am so sorry for not believing you. I don't know what was wrong with me." William apologized, held onto Mary, and kissed her forehead.

"Its okay hon. At least we are together again at last."

During the summer, Mary helped William find an apartment right near her house. By fall, Will started college and Mary started her senior year of high school. They went to all of the dances and they were always together. By the time Mary graduated, she moved in with her boyfriend.

CHAPTER THREE

A Cheater

Seven years past, Mary attended Lake Park Community College to start her writing career. William graduated from college in June with a Bachelor's degree in Criminal Justice. He got a part-time job at Sears working as a clerk. He was also in police school and was going to take the passing test next week to be certified as a police officer. Mary also worked part-time as a waitress at the Mall Diner.

It has been seven years since William and Mary have been dating. They couldn't have been any happier without each other in their lives.

It was a regular Tuesday morning, Will got ready for work while Mary worked on her second draft of the Star Sisters Two.

Mary sent her first Star Sisters book to Blue Light Publishing company in Chicago a couple of months ago. They loved the book and published it.

In the bedroom part of the apartment, William sat on the bed looking at a black box with a silver diamond ring in it.

"I can't believe that its been seven years since Mary and I have been together. We never had fights and no problems at all. I think its time for me to make our relationship into a full-term commitment. I want to ask Mary for her hand in marriage and I want to make this special for her and I'm going to ask her on her birthday next week." William looked at his desk calendar.

After he put the ring box back into his desk drawer, Will walked out into the living room where Mary was at.

"Hey, how's the book coming?" William wrapped his arms around her.

"The book is going well. I'm almost done editing and writing the second draft. I'm going to type the story next later on." Mary looked at her boyfriend.

"Cool. I can't believe in two weeks your book will come out and your birthday will be here too. I am so proud of you for accomplishing your dreams of being an author." William smiled and rubbed his girl's back.

"Thank you. I'm proud of you too. You are going to become a cop in a couple of weeks and you'll be quitting your job at the mall. I'm so happy for you!" Mary hugged William.

"I better get going to work. It's almost nine. I'll see you at five tonight." William grabbed his watch and wallet.

"Okay. I love you." Mary blew a kiss to William.

"I love you too babe."

Around four' thirty, William walked through Langston Park. He got off work early and do some thinking at the park.

"I think I will propose to Mary at the end of her special day. I'll have a little cake for Mary and I'll propose to her after she blows out the candles." William thought about Mary's birthday.

The next thing Will knew that he felt taps on his shoulder. He turned around to find a woman with light-brown hair and blue eyes behind him.

"Hi."

"Do I know you?" William asked the woman.

"You don't remember me Will? Its me Felicia Millerton, your ex-girlfriend."

"You! What are you doing here?" William with shock.

"The reason why I'm back in Lake Park is that I am here to fix my mistakes. While I was in Chicago with Josh, I finished high school and we were both supportive for each other until a month ago. I caught Josh with another girl in our apartment. He told me that he met her online and that we were fading away. I moved out a few days later and I came home." Felicia told the story to William.

"Oh well isn't that a shock." William didn't believe Felicia's story.

"Look, I figured out why Josh dumped me and it reminded me of what I did to you seven years ago on your graduation day when I dumped you for Josh. From the few days when I came home, I looked for you and all of your friends told me that you moved on and got back together with Mary Radcliffe. They also told me to stay away from you and that I was crazy to come back to you, but I'm not."

"You're wasting your time, because I am happy with Mary. She made me realize that I needed to get my life back together and she was there for me when I needed help. I've changed now. I've forgotten my old ways and I started with a clean slate. I love Mary and we've been together for seven years." William told Felicia about Mary.

"I know I was a fool to dump you and after all this time, I still have feelings for you. I really want to be your girlfriend again if you let me and I hope I still have a chance with you. I promise you that I'll be completely faithful to you and I'll never cheat on you again." Felicia begged William for another chance.

"I'm sorry Felicia, but I can't. The only person who has my heart is Mary. I can't be with you anymore. I love Mary with all my heart and I'm going to ask her to marry me on her birthday." William turned Felicia down and stayed faithful to Mary.

"What if you can test the both of us to see if who's the one that is faithful, who loves you, and who is meant for you?" Felicia gave an idea to William and touched his shirt.

"I don't know Felicia. I don't want to hurt Mary again like I did in the past. I don't want to lose her again."

"Maybe this will change your mind." Felicia grew closer to William and kissed him straight on the lips just like how she used to kiss him.

William didn't push Felicia away from him, he just let her kiss him. Forgetting Mary and falling under Felicia's spell.

She continued to kiss him long and passionately until she let go.

"Well, what's your answer Will?" Felicia, seductively touched William's face and stroked his hair.

"Yes and I will test you and Mary to see who is the girl that is meant for me. Oh Felicia, I missed you so much! I thought you'd never come back to me. I was lost without your love, but now you found me!" William dazed, happy, held Felicia in his arms, and swung her in the air.

"Oh Will!" Felicia looked into her boyfriend's eyes.

"Oh Felicia!" William looked into his second girlfriend's eyes and kissed her deeply.

Wednesday, August fourteenth, 2015, it's been one week since William saw Felicia. Their secret affair grew more and more serious everyday. Will spent the days with Mary and spent the nights with Felicia.

Mary didn't notice her boyfriend's absence, because she spent more time working on the Star Sisters sequel. That same afternoon, Mary worked on the fifth chapter of the book when her cell phone went off.

"Hello?" Mary answered her phone.

"Hey Mare, its Kaylin. How's it going?"

"Hi Kaylin, how've you been?"

"I've been doing great. School's going well. I have an audition for a play called Summer Days in Chicago on Friday." Kaylin told the story to Mary.

"That's great Kaylin, congratulations! You are living your dreams." Mary, happily to Kaylin.

"Thanks Mary. Oh, I heard your first book is coming out in three days. Congratulations!"

"Thanks Kaylin. I feel so happy that I am making something out of myself and having someone that loves me for who I am."

"How is William? What has he been up to lately?"

"William is okay. He's still working at the mall. He's almost done finishing up police academy at the college. He'll be taking the test soon to get certified. How's Eric?" Mary told everything to Kaylin.

"Eric is all right. He's still in school, learning how to open a tax paying business and he's working on his Associate's degree in Accounting." Kaylin told Mary her boyfriend's plans.

"That's great for Eric. Tell him I said hi for me."

"Sure. Tell William that we both said hi to him."

"I will. Hey, do you want to go out to a late lunch and catch up?"

"Sure. I'll meet you at the Vines of the Vineyard at two' thirty."

"Great, I'll see you then." Mary hung up her phone.

At the restaurant at two' thirty-five,

"Hey Mary, is that your boyfriend over there coming into the restaurant?" Kaylin looked at the entrance.

"Yeah, that's William. I didn't tell him that I was going out with you for lunch." Mary looked at the entrance.

"Did you write a note on the fridge saying you went out to lunch with me?"

"No, I didn't Kay. Why would he come to the restaurant unless there is a WOMAN!" Mary turned to find her boyfriend with another woman.

"You've got to be kidding Mare!" Kaylin continued to look at the entrance.

"Look, they're sitting by the café!"

"You know what, I'm going to the restroom and I'll spy on William. Maybe this mystery girl is one of his friends or family members." Kaylin got up from the table.

"I don't know Kay. I've seen all his friends and family members, but I never seen that girl before." Mary took a sip of her drink.

Kaylin walked over to the restroom and watched William and the mysterious woman.

"If William cheats on Mary and he hurts her, he will be dead meat for me and Eric!" Kaylin angrily thought and continued to walk.

A few minutes later as Kaylin walked back to the table, she saw William placed his arm around the woman and he kissed her everywhere.

"Of all the nerve!" Kaylin ran back to the table.

"Mary, come on, let's get out of here!" Kaylin grabbed her purse.

"What happened? What did you find out?"

"Your boyfriend is cheating on you! I saw him kissing that girl and holding her!" Kaylin told her friend everything.

"Oh my god! My own boyfriend is cheating on me! I have to get out of here quickly!" Mary panicked, grabbed her purse, and walked out of the dining room.

"Mary! Mary! Hold on for a second!" Kaylin ran out of the dining room after Mary.

By the café, Mary saw William talking and kissing the girl's hand. Tears ran down Mary's face as Kaylin helped her out of the restaurant.

At the apartment around three' thirty, Mary packed all her things in a couple of bags while Kaylin tried to calm her down.

"Mary, are you sure that you want to move out of the apartment?"

"Yes, I'm positive. I am done with William's lies! I have to get out of here so I can clear my head! Seven years down the drain!" Mary threw a picture of William holding her during Mary's twenty-fourth birthday last year into the garbage can.

"Why don't you move in with me and Eric until you are ready to get on your feet?" Kaylin offered Mary a place to stay.

"Thank you Kaylin, but I need to get out of Lake Park for a while. I'll go to South Hollow Wood and move in with Natalie and Scott. I promise once I come back to Lake Park, I will move in with you and Eric."

"Okay Mary, it's a deal. Listen, I have to call Eric. Good luck with Will and call me when you get to Natalie's."

"Thanks and don't worry, once William gets home, I will leave him, and get out of here!" Mary packed her last bag with her writing stuff.

"Oh, take care of yourself Mare. I'm going to miss you!" Kaylin hugged Mary.

"I know. I'm going to miss you too." Mary cried again.

"I will come and visit you in South Hollow Wood Mary, I promise. I'll see you some other time okay." Kaylin let go of her friend.

"I will. Bye Kaylin."

"Bye Mary." Kaylin walked out of the apartment.

Mary looked at the front door for a couple of minutes and went back to the bedroom to pack the rest of her stuff.

A half and hour later, Mary heard the front door open; she came out with her backpack to find William looking at the pile of bags by the door.

"Hey hon, how are you?" William hugged his girl.

"Don't give me that crap Will! I know what you are up to!" Mary pushed Will away.

"What do you mean by that Mary?" William, puzzled and with fear.

"You are cheating on me with another woman and after I gave you everything to help you turn your life around!"

"I'm not cheating Mary! You are overreacting!" William lied to Mary.

"You're lying to me! Today, I saw you at the Vines of the Vineyard while I was catching up with an old friend of mine with a girl that I didn't know and you had yourself all over her! Who is she William! Who is she?" Mary demanded as tears poured down her face.

There was a long pause within the room as William stared into Mary's eyes. He had to tell her the truth about Felicia and his affair with her.

"Mary, I need to tell you the truth. Last Tuesday, I was walking through Langston Park since I got off from work early and I bumped into my ex-girlfriend, Felicia Millerton. She looked for me, because she wanted me back as her boyfriend after she was dumped by her boyfriend in Chicago. So I decided to test you and Felicia to see who's the right girl for me. Since Tuesday, I've been having an affair with Felicia. That's why I haven't been home for the past few nights, because I spent the night with Felicia."

Mary stood there in tears, thinking the things that William did to Felicia and what Felicia did to William to prove their love for each other. That sickened Mary to her stomach that she couldn't bear to look at William.

"I'm leaving William, for good!" Mary walked to the door and grabbed her bags.

"Mary, please don't go! I already made my decision and it's you!" William tried to stop Mary from leaving.

"I don't want to hear it William! It's over for good! I am going to South Hollow Wood to live with Natalie and Scott until I get things together. I thought you were different William, but I guess I was wrong. Looks like you won't change. You will just be a cheater and a troublemaker forever. Goodbye William Valmont, forever!" Mary opened the door, grabbed her bags, and left.

CHAPTER FOUR

Death

William stood in the room looking at the hallway after Mary left. *"What are you standing here for? Go find Mary and tell her how much you love her so you can marry her!"* William's conscious told him to win Mary back.

"You're right. What was I thinking? Sacrificing my relationship with Mary for a meaningless affair with Felicia. I have to go find Mary before she leaves Lake Park forever!" William, guilty and he ran to the elevators.

The elevators were all full as William ran to the nearest stairwell and headed to the main hall. He was near the entrance doors when he bumped into Felicia.

"Will, where are you going in such a hurry?" Felicia asked William as he ran right past her.

"I can't talk to you right now Felicia. I have to find Mary. She's leaving me!" William panicked.

"So I guess that just leaves you and me. I'm the one that is meant for you!" Felicia bursted with happiness and ran into William's arms.

"No, no you are not the one I love!" William pushed Felicia away.

"What? Why? What do you mean that I'm not the one you love? It's Mary isn't it? You love her more than me!"

"Yes, I do love Mary more than you! She has been there for me when I needed help in my life while you went behind my back and cheated on me!" William told the truth to Felicia.

"I can't believe that you are saying this to me! I can't believe you used me and lied to me!" Felicia said as tears began to run down her face.

"No I didn't! You took advantage of me and I made a huge mistake about this test! I was so stupid for having this affair happen in the first place. You know, I was happy with Mary until you came back into my life! I had my life right and I was about to start to have my family with Mary until you crashed it! Face it Felicia, I have no feelings for you and even if we did get married, I wouldn't be happy with you. You would always cheat on me! I moved on and I don't want to be with you anymore! It's over between us for good!" William gave his word and ran to his car to catch Mary.

Felicia felt stupid, used, unneeded, and heartbroken that she lost the love of her life to someone who was much better for him.

"I can't believe William chose Mary over me! I guess it was a mistake for me to come back home and win back the man I love. I guess I will never find love again!" Felicia looked at the door.

Suddenly, Felicia felt sick and headed to the nearest restroom.

Meanwhile, Mary drove on route thirty-one that led out of Lake Park, into the village of Hillcrest, and into the city of South Hollow Wood. All the things that happened today swirled in Mary's head as she cried and continued to drive along Terrace Road (Route thirty-one).

William, who was not too far behind, followed Mary. He had to win her back and forget the things he did with Felicia and start the life he wants with Mary.

In the woods outside of Lake Park, Mary noticed William's car behind her and pulled her car over inside an empty street intersection. William pulled his car a couple of feet away from the street.

"Mary, thank goodness you finally stopped." William got out of the car.

"Why are you following me? I told you its over between us!" Mary walked up to William.

"Mary, I followed you, because I don't want to lose you." William took Mary's hands and begged her to stay with him.

"Why? So you can cheat on me again!" Mary snatched her hands back.

"No, I won't Mary. I was so stupid to fall for Felicia again. I am so sorry for doing that to you. Can you forgive me, Mary?" William begged for Mary's forgiveness.

"You should've tried harder William. I'm sorry, but I don't forgive you. After I helped you turn your life around and start fresh, but I guess I was wasting my time." Mary turned around and walked back to her car.

"Please Mary; I won't ever hurt you again. I promise to be completely faithful to you." William ran up to Mary's car, placed his hands on the car window, and banged on the window.

"Go away!" Mary yelled and tried to start the car, but it wouldn't start.

After ten minutes Mary stopped, broke into tears, and placed her head onto the steering wheel.

William stopped banging on the window, looked at his girlfriend for a couple of minutes, and left the car. William walked back to his car, heartbroken that he'll never have another chance with Mary again.

Suddenly, a car came down the street where Mary's car blocked the intersection. A woman in the other car was very drunk along with her three friends (who were also drinking) came down the hill fast.

Mary looked up and noticed the speeding car. She tried to start her car, but it wouldn't start as Mary panicked even more as the other car came towards her. It was too late; the speeding car crashed into Mary's car and carried her to a tree.

William saw the crash and panicked. He called 911 from his cell phone and ran to Mary's car.

"There's been an accident! I need an ambulance here right away! A car just crashed into my girlfriend's car and she can't get out! We're on route thirty-one outside of Lake Park!" William gave all the information to the 911 operator.

"Okay. We got all the information. We will send out a paramedic unit to the site now." The 911 operator told Will.

"Okay, thank you." William hung up and looked inside Mary's car.

Inside, Mary was pinned against the steering wheel unconscious and her head bleeding.

"Mary, Mary! I'm going to get you out of here, I promise!" William's eyes watered as he opened the car door.

Will pulled the seat back and carefully took Mary out of the car. He carried Mary to a grassy area just before a small fire started inside the two cars. William did CPR for five minutes until he heard breathing sounds from Mary's mouth.

"Mary, you are going to be fine. I'm right here at your side, I'm not going anywhere, and I'm not leaving you. The ambulance is on the way to help you." William held his bleeding girlfriend in his arms.

Mary looked scared and tearful at Will. Her head was bleeding heavily, her body was crushed, and couldn't move.

"Why did you save me?"

William couldn't hear Mary's words that he leaned towards her to hear the question.

"I saved your life Mary, because I love you. I have always loved you and I'm not going to let anything happen to you." William professed his love to Mary.

Mary just looked at her boyfriend with her tear-dried bloody face as her face watered fresh new tears. Mary felt happy that William loves her, but still upset that he cheated on her for his ex-girlfriend. The things that Felicia and William did together kept on going through Mary's head. Inside, Mary was dying and crying that she fell into unconsciousness.

"Mary, Mary! Please don't do this to me now!" William performed CPR on Mary until the paramedics arrived.

At Sheridan Memorial Hospital back in Lake Park, the paramedics revived Mary to a weakened condition. They brought her into Trauma room two of the emergency room as Doctor Henderson operated on her. Mary lost hope and her life.

William, behind the trauma room doors in shock, crying, praying, and hoped that Mary will pull through. He watched as his girlfriend was hooked onto an oxygen tube and her body was cut open. Mary, awake and very frightened and looked at William. They both looked at each other and cried together.

"Give me some morphine and two grams of anesthetic so I can put Mary to sleep before heading to surgery." Dr. Henderson tried to stop the bleeding.

Mary looked up at the ceiling staring into the lights in pain and thinking.

"It looks like my life has come to an end. I never knew that betrayal and pain killed me in the end. William made his decision and he chose Felicia while I was left to be alone. I choose to die and not be here as the future unfolds." Mary made her decision, the decision to die.

Suddenly, Mary went into a cardiac arrest.

"Doctor, we just lost her heartbeat!" The nurse looked at the heart monitor.

"Okay, hand me the paddles! Charge it up to two hundred! Ready! Clear!" Dr. Henderson tried to revive Mary.

William couldn't bear to see Mary on the gurney that he walked over to the waiting room and waited for Mary to come out.

"Charge it up to three hundred and clear!" Dr. Henderson shocked Mary for the fifth time.

"Doctor, I think you should call it, because I don't think she's here anymore." The nurse stopped CPR.

"Okay, I'll call it. Time of death, 5:07PM. Was there anyone that came with her?" Dr. Henderson took off his gloves and turned off the heart monitor.

"Yes, her boyfriend is here. He's waiting in the waiting room." The nurse took off the oxygen mask.

"All right. I better tell him the news." Dr. Henderson walked out of the trauma room.

William sat in a chair, trying to calm down when Dr. Henderson came in.

"Mr. Valmont, I have some bad news. Your girlfriend, Mary Radcliffe didn't make it."

"What?" William fell into complete despair after he got up from his chair.

"She had very little life in her when we were operating on her. She was crushed and she lost a lot of blood after the crash. It seemed like she wanted to die after she found out something disturbing and wanted to die after she found out the upsetting news."

"Oh my god! Mary's dead! No, it can't be! I don't believe it!" William panicked, cried, and couldn't control it.

"I am so sorry for your loss Mr. Valmont. Would you like to see her before we move her to the morgue?"

"Yes, I would like to see her." William wiped his face and tried to cheer up.

In Trauma room 2, Mary was left with a ghostly figure. The oxygen tube was gone and her eyes closed.

"I'll leave you alone to say your goodbyes to your girlfriend." Dr. Henderson left the room.

William looked at Mary's body with despair.

"Why did you go Mary? Why did you have to leave me? I was going to ask you to marry me, start our lives together, and raise our family together. Mary, I am so sorry for hurting you. I didn't mean to hurt you. I wish that I didn't have that stupid affair with Felicia! I wish you were still alive so we could be together." William cried and took Mary's hand, apologized to her, kissed her hand and forehead, and left the room guilty that he killed his only true love.

CHAPTER FIVE

Another Chance

Three days later on Saturday, August 17th, 2015 was Mary's birthday and the day of her funeral. Every one of Mary's friends and family members were in town to attend Mary's funeral. The funeral took place at Rose Hill Cemetery and the memorial party was at Mary's childhood home.

"As we mourn the loss of this beloved young woman, we look deep within ourselves to think who would bring this woman's life at such a tragic end. We all know that Mary is in a better place now, looking down at us, and watching us. Mary Radcliffe, you will be truly missed." Father Peter performed the ceremony.

William looked at Mary with deep misery. She was dressed in a pink dress with her hair down, straightened and half-curled. Mary was beautiful even though she was dead.

Everyone got up and placed a pink rose onto Mary's closed coffin. Natalie and Kaylin were the only ones left to place their flowers onto Mary's casket as everyone headed to the Radcliffe house for the memorial.

"I can't believe that William did this to our best friend!" Natalie wept and placed the rose onto the casket.

"I know Natalie, I know. Don't worry, he's going to pay for betraying our friend!" Kaylin, angrily looked at the casket.

"After Mary gave up most of her life helping William get his life together, he goes back to his old ways and cheats on her for the low-down slut Felicia." Natalie turned away from the coffin.

"Come on, let's go to the party. Everyone is waiting for us." Kaylin took Natalie to her car.

At the Radcliffe house, Petra threw a special memorial party in honor for her daughter on her birthday.

"Mrs. Radcliffe, I am so sorry for your loss. Mary meant the world to us and we loved her more than anything in the world." William hugged Petra.

"Thank you William. You took care of my loving daughter with love and respect, She was lucky to be with you Will. You were always there for her and you loved her very much. You will always be a son to our family." Petra looked at William.

"Thank you Mrs. Radcliffe for making me a part of your family. Mary would have loved it." William felt guilty as he looked at Mary's mother.

"Look at him, being all sorry for Mary's mother when deep inside, he's happy that Mary is dead!" Kaylin, with disgust to Eric.

"He doesn't give a crap about Mary at all!" Jeremy through his folded hands.

"I could just kick his ass right now!" Eric exclaimed.

"Oh god no! Please don't tell me that William's slutty girlfriend is crashing Mary's party!" Elisa in shock after Felicia walked into the house.

"How dare Felicia come barging in on Mary's special day on her birthday!" Natalie looked at Felicia with fury as she hugged Scott.

"How dare William choose Felicia over Mary? She's just a wild, guy hopping slut!" Susan in anger and disgust.

"Oh boy, here comes trouble." Tyler consoled Susan as William walked towards Mary's friends.

William felt a familiar touch of taps on his shoulder. He turned around to find Felicia behind him.

"Hey." Felicia, sweetly looked at her boyfriend.

"What the hell are you doing here Felicia? At my girlfriend's funeral!" William angrily to Felicia.

"Look, there is something I need to tell you about what I found out just a couple of days ago." Felicia explained her story.

"I don't want to talk to you right now. I have a lot to deal with right now and the last person that I want to talk to is you." William walked past Felicia.

"But Will; we need to talk about us and my news!" Felicia followed William.

"Well look who it is. It's William and his trashy girlfriend! I should've known that I'd smelt something fishy coming by!" Natalie, angrily at William and Felicia.

"Natalie, you guys, can I talk to you for a couple of minutes?" William begged to talk to Mary's friends.

"Why? So we can end up like Mary, dead and buried!" Scott, angrily and held Natalie.

"No. I just wanted to apologize to you guys for what I've done."

"Well, why don't you apologize to Mary and bring her back to life! You killed our best friend William. You and your slutty girlfriend finished her!" Kevin walked up to Will with anger.

"If you try to apologize to us, we will never forgive you for what you done to our Mary!" Kaylin sobbed.

"Come on guys, let's go before I get even sicker!" Noah led everyone away from William, and walked to the backyard.

"You know, back in high school, I should've setup Mary with her old friend Harry Jordan. They would've been a great couple." Susan cried on Tyler's shoulder.

"I know, but she chose that unfaithful jerk!" Scott tried to cheer up his girlfriend.

"Good, they finally leave! Will, I am sorry for what happened to Mary, but I need to talk about our relationship and my news." Felicia looked at William.

"You're not sorry Felicia. You wanted this to happen. I wanted to propose to Mary, but you ruined it! I am so stupid for ever hooking up with you again!"

"Please Will, don't say that! We can talk this out just you and me."
Felicia touched William's face and tried to calm him down.

"No! I don't want to talk to you Felicia! Just stay the hell away from
me! Just stay away, forever! I only wanted Mary, not you!" William
walked away from Felicia.

"No Will, please wait!" Felicia tried to stop William, but he ignored
her and continued to walk away.

*"Great! Now I can't tell Will that I am carrying his child. I guess that he
doesn't care about me anymore. I was right… I was just wasting my time trying
to win Will back. I'm never going to find the right guy for me when he doesn't
even want me!"* Felicia, in tears and ran out of Mary's house.

At the apartment that evening, William looked through some of
Mary's things before he packed them into boxes and bring them back to
her parents. Earlier that day, the newspapers released an advertisement
for The Star Sisters in stores today after seven in the morning.

William looked at the paper and packed it with the rest of Mary's
writing things. He found a couple of Mary's journals on the top shelf in
the closet. The journals were dated back to Mary's years in junior high
and high school. William read through one journal when Mary was
in her eighth grade year of school. One page talked about the surprise
visit William made one day at Leavenston.

"Friday, April tenth, 2004,

*Today was such a wonderful day for me. I was called down to the office
during seventh period. I thought I gotten myself into trouble, but I was wrong.
When I got to the office, I was surprised to see William in the office sitting there.
He came up to me and hugged me so hard that I thought I was going to explode
into him! He stayed with me until school was finished. William took me to the
mall for two hours before he took me home. I had such a wonderful day today
and tomorrow will be even better when William takes me to the Sweetheart
dance at the community center."* Mary's journal stated as Will continued
to read it.

William flipped to the last page of the diary and saw a list Mary
made.

"These are my goals in my life that I would like to accomplish in my life.

Goal #1: I would like to be a Teacher
I would like to teach knowledge to people and help them in anyway. I would love to teach to first or second graders.

Goal #2: I would like to be an Author
Since I was little, I loved to write stories. I write about everything. I take my ideas that I create in my head and form them into stories. I want to be a successful writer someday and I hope that my successful books will become movies.

Goal #3: I would like to be a Perfect Wife
When I settle down someday, I want to be a wife who never makes mistakes to her family. I want to have a husband who will never betray me or even cheat on me. I would like to have two or three kids with my future husband.

Goal #4: I would like to be a Singer
I love to sing. Ever since third grade and taking music classes, I just love to sing. I sometimes like to write lyrics and songs, but most of the time its complicated. I would like to form a band with a bunch of my friends or be a solo singer. Who knows…

Goal #5: I would like to be a Nurse's Assistant
I like to become a Nurse's Assistant in a doctor's office, because I love to help people when they are sick or injured. I would be a great nurse's assistant to help cure diseases to save people's lives.
These are the dreams and goals that I want to have in my life. Who knows, maybe I can accomplish all of them before my life ends." Mary's journal described as William read through the list.

After reading the journal, William placed it into a box labeled, "Mary's things". He picked up Mary's journal from her senior year of high school when they got back together.
"Tuesday, May first, 2008,
I can't believe it's finally May! Graduation is almost here as well as prom. I finally got the tickets last week and I can't wait to go to the prom with William! The dance will be magical with Will there. I want him to have a great time with me this year than last year. Even though he risked his prom last year to come

over to my house and dance with me in my backyard, I knew he was the one. Especially when he was in a black suit and a green tie and I was in my pink nightgown. William is always good to me. He always calls, he comes every night to my house to check on me, and he surprises me with gifts whenever I am sad or happy. I love him so much that I can't stop thinking about him half the time. I'm glad that we are together again and last year's troubles have melted away."

William cried after reading the entry. He laid down on the bed that he and Mary shared together.

"Mary, I wish you were still here with me. I wish I could change the past so I can bring you back from the dead." William ached for Mary.

"I can help you bring back your girlfriend to life." A voice called to William.

"What? Who's there?" William jumped up.

"I can help you bring your girlfriend back to life."

"Who's that?" William with confusion and looked around the room.

"I'm over here, behind you!" The voice called to William.

William turned around to find an angel in the room by the window.

"Who are you?"

"My name is Gabrielle and I'm an angel. You know, you really hurt your girlfriend Mary when you told her about your affair with your ex-girlfriend."

"I know. I feel so guilty for making that mistake that I shouldn't have… Hey, wait a minute! How do you know about this situation?"

"I was in the living room when you told Mary about your affair with Felicia, I was in the car with Mary when the accident happened, and I was with her at the hospital when she died. You know, she actually wanted to die, because she didn't want to see you dump her, spend the rest of your life with Felicia Millerton, and you getting hurt by her all the time."

"Oh, why did I deserve this? Losing my one true love!" William collapsed on his bed and placed his hands over his face.

"You know, I can bring Mary back, but you will have to complete a mission in order to bring Mary whole and alive again." Gabrielle told William good news.

"What do I have to do?" William, suddenly looked up.

"Can I see Mary's eighth grade journal for a second?"

William went back into the box, brought out the purple journal, and gave it to Gabrielle.

Gabrielle flipped open the diary and found the page where Mary's goals were written down.

"William, your mission is to find five orbs from Mary's dream goals in her life. The dreams and goals will come alive forming Mary in alternate worlds. You on the other hand, hurt Mary before her dreams began. You have to repair the relationship with Mary as a friend, girlfriend, or fiancée in order to get the orb." Gabrielle closed the book.

"So, all I have to do is to collect the orbs of my girlfriend's dreams in her future, repair the relationship with her, and she'll be alive again."

"Yes, she will be alive. You will get your chance to propose to Mary and to start a life with her."

"Okay, I'll do it." William accepted the plan.

"Great! Now, we are going back in time when Mary graduated high school and you left her for someone else." Gabrielle told William what was going to happen.

"Okay. What goal will I encounter first?"

"You will encounter Mary as her dream of becoming a Nurse's Assistant. I will help you along your journey. If you need a hand, I'll be there." Gabrielle took William and they teleported from the bedroom.

CHAPTER SIX

Mary, A Nurse

Gabrielle took William back two years to the year 2013 where Mary was twenty-three years old and still lived in Lake Park.

"Where are we?" William looked around his surroundings.

"We are in Mary's apartment in her nursing career."

William walked over to a table by a sofa and picked up a picture of Mary and another man with his arms around her.

"Gabrielle, who is this guy holding my girlfriend?" William looked at the picture with disgust.

"Oh William, this is Mary's fiancé, Matt Branson." Gabrielle told William the bad news.

"What?" William, in shock.

"Yes. You see, Mary met Matt in college while Mary studied her degree in Medical Assisting. They dated for two years until Christmas, Matt proposed to Mary and accepted his marriage proposal."

"Oh my god, I lost Mary! I really lost her now." William placed the picture back on the table, sat on the sofa, and placed his face in his hands.

"No, you didn't lose her yet. In two days, you will walk up to Mary's doorstep and come back into her life. Come on, let's go to the apartment that you are sharing with Kathryn Erison."

Mary's apartment disappeared and they were left in a black room.

"What! I live with Kathryn Erison! I hardly even know her! All I know is that she's engaged to my friend James." William, suddenly with shock.

"Well in this world, you are with Kathryn." Gabrielle told William as they looked at a flashback.

It was Friday, May eighteenth, 2007, William cleaned out his school locker. After he closed the door, Kathryn Erison stood there.

"Hey Will, can I talk to you for a couple of minutes?"

"Yeah, what is it?" William with concern.

"Well, ever since I transferred here to Lake Park high, I developed a crush on you. I wanted to tell you this so I can be your girlfriend, but I was afraid to tell you."

"Look Kathryn, I have a girlfriend and I love her very much. I'm sorry, but I can't be with you." William turned Kathryn down.

"But, I love you more than your girlfriend does!" Kathryn declared her love.

"Okay. I'll break up with Mary so that I can be with you." William made a deal with Kathryn.

"Thank you William thank you! I promise that you'll never regret this." Kathryn happily leaped into Will's arms.

The flashback stopped where William held Kathryn as Gabrielle and William came into view.

"Oh, how stupid was I to dump Mary for Kathryn, even though I didn't like her." William with guilt.

"Yeah, you did. Let's look ahead at your graduation party two weeks afterwards. After two times of going out on dates with Kathryn, you started to like her and forgot all about Mary."

It was Saturday, May twenty-third, 2007, the day of William's graduation. Mary, Susan, Ed, and Kaylin attended the graduation and went to Will's house for the party. Mary looked for William all over the house until she found him in the backyard with Kathryn.

"There you are babe! I've been looking for you everywhere. Where have you been?" Mary hugged Will.

"Mary, we need to talk about our relationship." William let go of Mary.

"What do you mean?" Mary with concern.

"You see, for the last two weeks we've been drifting apart and I've started to fall in love with someone else. I'm sorry Mare, but I'm breaking up with you for Kathryn Erison." William held Kathryn's hand.

"What? How could you do this to me!" Mary with shock.

"Look Mary, Kathryn told me that she had a crush on me since she moved to Lake Park high. So, I decided to go out with her and dump you." William held Kathryn in his arms.

"I can't believe that you are doing this to me! After I gave you everything in my life, but you go onto the next best thing!" Mary cried.

"Hey Mary, it's getting late. Let's go home!" Tyler yelled for Mary as Susan and Kaylin came out into the backyard.

"Mary, are you okay? What's wrong?" Susan noticed her friend crying.

"William is dumping me for Kathryn Erison!" Mary sobbed through her tears.

"What?" Kaylin looked at Kathryn and William with shock.

"Will, how could you do this to Mary?" Susan asked for an explanation.

"Mary couldn't love me as much as Kathryn loves me. That's why I'm going out with Kathryn and leaving Mary." William looked into Kathryn's eyes.

"You know what Will, you stay away from Mary! You stay away from her forever!" Tyler pushed William.

"Stop it! Don't you dare hurt my boyfriend!" Kathryn protected William and pushed Tyler.

"Your boyfriend! You took William away from Mary you skank!" Kaylin pushed Kathryn.

"Excuse me!" Kathryn with anger.

"You heard me! Want a piece of me? Then come and get it!" Kaylin continued to push Kathryn until she fell to the ground.

"All right that's enough Kaylin! Leave Kathryn alone! Just keep Mary away from me forever! Come on Kathryn, let's go pack my stuff and get out of this town like we planned." William rushed to Kathryn's side, lifted her into his arms, and carried her off into the house, kissing her along the way.

"Mary, let's get out of here! You deserve much better than that William Valmont!" Susan took Mary out of the yard.

The flashback paused where Susan helped a devastated Mary and faded back into the dark room.

"I can't believe that I did that to Mary. I just can't believe it!" William, after he looked at the flashback.

"I know. You were selfish and left Mary out of everything, but you realized that you still have feelings for Mary after a few years of being with Kathryn. You were at the grocery store when you ran into one of Mary's friends a couple of days ago." Gabrielle took William into another flashback.

It was Sunday, March, twenty-ninth, 2013, William was at Greenland Supermarket in the Produce aisle when he recognized a familiar face.

"Susan Kittle? Is that you?"

Susan turned around to find William Valmont behind her.

"William Valmont? Is that you? You haven't changed much over the last six years." Susan, stunned while she looked at William.

"I know. Hey, what are you doing here in Sunnydale?"

"Well, I decided to go to Layola University to advance my medical career as a Hospice Nurse. Noah Washell and I moved here a year after we transferred out of Lake Park Community College. What about you? Are you still with Kathryn Erison?" Susan told William what she did over the years.

"Yes, I'm still with Kathryn. I thought about proposing to her, but something is bothering me. It's about Mary. Is she okay? How is she doing?"

"Oh, Mary is doing fine. She's still living in Lake Park. The last time I talked to her, she graduated college and working full-time at Doctor Samson's office. You know William before I left Lake Park, Mary told me that she misses you a lot and she thinks about you everyday. She also told me that it was all her fault for losing you and not loving you enough." Susan told William what Mary did the past six years.

"Really, she misses me?" William, with concern.

"Yes and deep down inside her, she still loves you."

"Oh man, I really broke Mary's heart for the worst." William, with guilt.

"Yes you did break Mary's heart big time. You better think hard before asking the big question to Kathryn. Anyways, I'll see you around William." Susan warned William and walked away.

The flashback stopped and faded back into the black room.

"After your run in with Susan, you realized that deep down inside, you still loved Mary more than Kathryn. Now, this is where you make your decision. Either you stay in Sunnydale and propose to Kathryn or go back to Lake Park to win Mary back. Who will you choose?" Gabrielle asked William as his bedroom came into focus.

"I guess I do have to make a decision." William sat on the bed and picked up a picture of Mary.

"I will leave you to make your choice." Gabrielle disappeared.

"I can't believe you William!" Kathryn walked into the room with anger.

"What did I do?" William panicked and hid the picture of Mary underneath his pillow.

"Why do you have pictures of you ex-girlfriend Mary Radcliffe in your sock drawer?" Kathryn looked at the pictures with disgust and threw them all over the room.

"I...I..."

"Tell me huh, you still love her do you? Answer the question!" Kathryn, with rage.

"To tell you the truth Kathryn, I'm still in love with Mary Radcliffe. I'm not happy here and it was a big mistake to leave her for you. I'm going back to Lake Park and win Mary back." William told the truth to Kathryn.

"You know what, you're right Will. Just go back to Lake Park and win back the girl you love! I don't know why I ran off with you Will. I guess, I wasn't thinking straight. I was crazy and in love with you. Now please, pack your things, and get out of my apartment!" Kathryn cried and left the room.

William packed all his things together, got into his car, and left Sunnydale forever.

It took William two hours from Sunnydale to Lake Park. He checked into the Lakeview hotel to live there temporally until he can live on his own.

Meanwhile, Mary enjoyed her life. She worked at Sheridan Memorial Hospital. Mary had a lot of people she could look up to.

There was Elizabeth Peterson. She's a nurse at the office. She met Mary at Lake Park Community College while she studied her Nursing degree. They became good friends since all of Mary's old friends moved out of town and started their lives, except for Jessie Sootburg and Tyler Hagerton.

They stayed behind to help Mary with her life ever since William left. Tyler and Jessie were happy that Mary moved on with her life with Matt Branson.

Matt met Mary on a blind date with Tyler and Jessie. After the night ended, Matt and Mary were a couple. He attended Lake Park community College to get his degree in Teaching. Right now, Matt is a substitute teacher at Kempford Junior High School.

On Friday, March twenty-seventh, 2013, there was a new Nurse's Assistant in Doctor Samson's office, Her name is Nadine Colesen.

Mary introduced herself to Nadine and the rest of her co-workers. Nadine got along with everyone on her first day.

Monday, March thirtieth, 2013, Mary was at the office, unaware that a surprise was waiting for her.

"So Mary, how many patients we have until we have our break?" Nadine filled out a patient chart.

"Um actually, we only have one patient left. Don't worry Nadine, I'll take care of this patient." Mary took a patient chart from the daily patient box.

"Thanks Mary. You are a lifesaver." Nadine winked at Elizabeth, who winked back at Nadine.

"Beth Alder, the doctor would like to see you now." Mary called for Beth.

Instead of Beth Alder, it was Matt with a bouquet of pink roses.

"Oh my god, Matt! What are you doing here? Shouldn't you be at work?" Mary, with surprise.

"Well, I didn't have to go to work today. So, I decided to come see you at work and take you out to lunch." Matt gave the flowers to his fiancee.

"Awww, this is so sweet of you Matt! Sure, I would love to go out to lunch with you. I'll check myself out for my lunch break." Mary happily kissed Matt.

Meanwhile back at the Lakeview hotel, William looked through the newspaper trying to find an apartment.

He found a nice apartment downtown that has furniture, low-priced utilities, and rent is only 107 a month. He immediately called the number listed at the bottom of the ad.

"Hello Ms. Elmtree, I am William Valmont and I'm interested on the apartment you listed in the paper."

"Mr. Valmont, why don't you come down to the apartment complex tomorrow and I'll have you fill out some paperwork and we'll see if you're qualified for the apartment."

"Okay then. What time would you like me to come tomorrow?"

"You can come around three O' clock for the appointment."

"Great, I'll see at three tomorrow." William hung up the phone.

That same night, William looked up Mary's address in the phone book. He found out that Mary lived near the apartment that he was going to move in tomorrow.

Tuesday around three in the afternoon, William checked out of the Lakeview hotel and went to the penthouse apartment buildings on Red Tail Drive. After filling out some forms, Ms. Elmtree looked over the paperwork.

"Well Mr. Valmont, after looking at your information you are the perfect person for the apartment." Ms. Elmtree shook William's hand.

"Thank you Ms. Elmtree. Thank you very much!" William received the key.

Ms. Elmtree gave Will the tour around apartment 308 and once she left.

Around five that evening, William left his apartment to go see Mary.

On White Dove Lane, William walked into the building to the directory. William looked at the directory and found Mary's name.

After getting off the elevator, William walked down the hallway towards 217.

Mary, who come home early from work was sitting on the couch talking to Elizabeth (who had the day off) on the phone when she heard the doorbell rang.

"Hey, Elizabeth, I'll call you back later. Someone's at the door. It could be Matt." Mary got up from the couch.

"Okay Mary, I'll talk to you later." Elizabeth hung up.

Mary put the phone down and answered the door. She opened the door to find William Valmont at her door.

Everything came back to Mary while she looked at William's face. The day of his graduation party, the day he dumped Mary for Kathryn, ran out of Lake Park with Kathryn and Mary left in the dust, heartbroken and abandoned. Mary snapped out of the flashbacks and back into reality.

"William! What are you doing here?" Mary, with a serious, angry look on her face.

"Mary, I know you are angry and surprised that I am at your apartment. I know that I ran off on you, dumped you for Kathryn, and I hurt you. I was so stupid for abandoning you and leaving you alone. I am so sorry for breaking your heart." William apologized to Mary.

"Are you telling me the truth?" Mary, with a serious look on her face as her anger disappeared from her face.

"Yes Mary, I am telling you the truth. That's why I came home to find you, apologize to you, and repair our relationship together." William looked straight into her eyes.

"Okay Will, I forgive you. Come on in, let's go into the kitchen and talk." Mary smiled.

CHAPTER SEVEN

Jealousy

"So Mary, what have you been up too since the last six years?" William sat at the kitchen table as Mary made coffee.

"Well, after you left town, I didn't know what to do with myself. I was heartbroken without you and devastated that you dumped me for Kathryn, took her in your arms, and you both left together in front of me and my friends. I thought that you would never do that to me, to hurt me or my life. So, I had to move on with my life without you." Mary poured coffee into two cups.

"Mary, I am so sorry for abandoning you. I wasn't thinking straight, I was selfish, and thinking about myself."

"I know you are sorry and I forgive you, but I had to move on with my life." Mary handed the cup to Will.

"What did you do after graduation?" William drank his coffee.

"Well, I went to college. I had nothing else to turn to. So, I decided to go to Lake Park Community College to get my Nursing career started. Mostly all of my friends moved out of Lake Park to start their lives except for Tyler Hagerton and Jessie Sootburg. They stayed here and helped me go to college and start my life over with a clean slate. After two years of being in college and made new friends, I earned my Nurse's Assistant license and degree. I got a job in Doctor Nora Samson's office at Sheridan Memorial Hospital. I achieved my dreams until you came back into my life again. William, why did you come back to Lake Park? Why?"

"Mary, the reason why I came back to home was that I missed you so much. Every day, I thought about you, I looked at pictures of you, and I couldn't get you off my mind. I wanted another chance with you and make you happy again. Will you please go out with me again?"

There was a long silence within the room. Mary looked at William in shock as he looked into Mary's eyes.

"Oh William... I... I can't!" Mary studdered.

"Why not?"

"I'm engaged to be married to Matt Branson. You see, while you were gone and I was in college, I met Matt after Tyler and Jessie set me up on a double date one Saturday night in December, 2009. We dated ever since that night and throughout college. Last year, Matt asked me to marry him and I accepted his proposal. I am sorry to tell you this William, but I'm taken."

"Mary... I have to get going. I have to go to a few places to get things for my new apartment." William studdered in shock as he got up from the chair.

"Of course you do." Mary doubted Will.

"It was nice seeing you again Mary. I'll probably come over some other time." William walked to the front door.

"Yeah, sure."

"I can't believe that I left Mary's place thinking of myself instead of saying that I'm happy that she's getting married."

The next thing he knew, white smoke filled the room and Gabrielle appeared.

"Hello William, how's the mission going?" Gabrielle sat on the couch with William.

"The mission is going horribly wrong. I am treating Mary like she's nothing. I asked her out, but then she turned me down. Then she told me about her fiance, Matt and that she was marrying him. After she told me her happy news, I turned selfish and I didn't say that I was happy for her." William, sadly to Gabrielle.

"I knew this was going to happen. William, you have to take it slow with Mary. I know that she is getting married, but you can't have the option of being Mary's boyfriend anymore." Gabrielle tried to cheer Will up.

"But I want to be her boyfriend! I want to have another chance with Mary! I want to tell her how much I still love her and care about her!" William threw papers all over the room in anger.

"I know that you are still in love with Mary, William, but she moved on with her life and found another person that is perfect for her. You have to just be friends with her and let Mary be with Matt."

"Okay, you are right. I should be Mary's friend. She deserves Matt in her life as her husband instead of me." William lied to Gabrielle.

"There are other missions that you will face where you will win Mary's heart. In this mission, you have to win Mary back as your friend and accept Mary's soon to be marriage to Matthew. All you have to do is wait." Gabrielle told William to be patient.

"All right, I'll give it a go with being Mary's friend. I better go apologize to her tomorrow when I go visit Mary at work." William surrendered and closed up his feelings for Mary.

"Great! I'll be watching to see how this all goes tomorrow." Gabrielle disappeared while William thought about what to say to Mary the next day.

Friday, Mary was at the office with Nadine since Elizabeth had another day off.

"What? That dingbat William Valmont came back to Lake Park last night to see you!" Nadine, with shock.

"Yes, he came back to apologize to me for what happened back when I was in high school." Mary told Nadine the story.

"Did you forgive him Mary?"

"Yes, I did." Mary answered Nadine's question.

"Why?"

"Sometimes, when people that you care about hurt you and they apologize to you, you always give them a second chance. I forgave William, because he knew that he hurt me so bad that he had to come back home and apologize to me in person for what he did to me." Mary explained what Will did.

"I see, I get what you mean. Did you tell Will about your engagement to Matt?"

"Yes I did Nadine." Mary filed records.

"Well, what did he say?"

"Well, William just freaked out about the engagement that he left the apartment after I told him about it."

"Oh no, you shouldn't have told William about the engagement Mary!" Nadine took a file from the cabinet.

"I... I... I had to tell him Nadine and besides, William had to find out sooner or later!"

"I know, but why do you think that William came back to Lake Park for you?" Nadine, with concern.

"I don't know Nadine. I really don't." Mary looked at her friend.

"I think the reason why William came back is that he wants to be with you. He wants another chance with you. Did he say that he broke up with Kathryn?"

"No, he didn't."

"Mary, there's a guy in the waiting room looking for you!"

"Okay, thanks Alisa. I'll be there in a minute. It's probably Matt taking me out to lunch again. I'll see you after lunch Nadine." Mary placed the files back into the cabinet.

"Have fun." Nadine placed medical papers into a file.

"William, what on earth are you doing here?" Mary walked out into the waiting room to find William there.

"Mary, I came down to apologize to you for what happened last night." William got up from a chair.

"I can't believe you are here."

"Mary, I am so sorry that I walked out on you last night and I wanted to make it up to you by taking you out to lunch on your break and catch up again, if you want to."

"Okay William, I forgive you and yes, I will go to lunch with you."

"Thank you Mary. You are an angel." William hugged Mary.

"I am always there for a friend. No matter what happens. Come on, I'm checked out and ready to go."

"Okay." William smiled as he walked after her.

"So Will, what happened to Kathryn?"

"Well, she threw me out of the apartment that we were living in after I told her that I still had feelings for you."

"Wow, she must have been stupid to be with you." Mary laughed.

"Yeah, she was. So Mary, tell me more about Matt Branson?"

"Matt is the same age as I am. Right now, he's a substitute teacher at Kempford Junior High and he's trying to get his Master's degree in teaching. He is just an awesome guy who is sweet and the nicest person you could ever meet in your life. He really did light up my life when I was dating him."

"Oh, I see. I can tell that he is the perfect guy for you. Um Mary, I need to tell you something." William, with sorrow.

"Yes, what is it?" Mary, with a look of concern.

"I know that I've hurt you in the past and I still have feelings for you. This is why I came back to Lake Park to find you and see you. Would you give me another chance to be with you? I promise to you Mary, that I will be better to you and make you happy like I used to make you. Please, I beg you, give up the life you plan to have with Matt and have a life with me." William took Mary's hand, held it, and looked into her eyes.

"Oh William, I..." Mary looked at Will.

"Mary, thank goodness I found you! I went to the office to see if you wanted to go out to lunch and discuss the wedding, but Alisa told me that you went to lunch with an old friend of yours." Matt hugged Mary after he walked into the cafe.

"Oh my god, I completely forgot that we had a lunch date today and wrap up on the wedding plans! I am so sorry, but an old friend of mine came into town two days ago and we were catching up. Matt, this is my good friend and ex-boyfriend, William Valmont. Will, this is my fiance and future husband, Matt Branson." Mary apologized and introduced her fiance to William.

"Oh, it's nice to finally meet you William." Matt put out his hand to Will.

"Likewise." William shook Matt's hand.

"Please Matt, join us so we can discuss the wedding."

"Yes, we will discuss the wedding honey. Don't worry about it. So, you were the one who broke my fiancee's heart back when she became a senior in high school." Matt calmed Mary down and sat down.

"I know I did hurt Mary and I apologized to her for leaving her."

"Thank you for apologizing to Mary. You know, Mary told me that you had a bad history and she helped you see the light to do good things in your life."

"Yes, Mary literally saved my life. You are lucky to deserve Mary in your life."

"She's an angel and that's why I'm marrying her." Matt put his arm around Mary and kissed her on the lips.

Matt continued to kiss Mary, William got angry and jealous at Matt inside that he wanted to kill Matt in front of Mary, but he snapped out of his kill state when he heard Mary's voice.

"Um Matt, I ordered the flowers for the bridesmaids and the church last night. Now, all we need to do is to pick out the food that is going to be served at the reception."

"What kinds of choices do we have for the dinner?"

"Well, we have the baked chicken with mashed potatoes and vegetables, catfish with baked potatoes and coleslaw, or roast beef with vegetables and rice."

"I was thinking of the baked chicken to serve as the main course."

"Okay and what about the soup? There's clam chowder soup, tomato soup, or the vegetable soup." Mary wrote in her wedding planner.

Meanwhile, William got sick and tired that he got up from the table and left the restaurant.

"I thought about the vegetable soup and the summer salad for the first course."

"Great, that takes care of everything." Mary wrote down the last thing in the planner and closed the book.

"Great, oh, I better get back to work. I'll see you at home tonight. Love you." Matt got up from the table and kissed Mary.

"Love you too. See you tonight. Now William, where were we?" Mary turned to find William gone.

"William, where did you go?" Mary looked for Will.

"I can't believe that William Valmont! First, he wants to be nice with me and then he takes off before I can trust him! That's why he left in the first place, because he couldn't trust me at all! I don't know why I put up with him or try to give him another chance anyways?" Mary paid the bill, left a tip on the table, and left the café.

As Mary walked back up to the hospital, she didn't hear sniffling noises coming from the abandoned alleyway behind the café, William cried as he watched Mary go back to the hospital.

"Maybe it was a mistake for me to come home. I guess I can't win a loveship or even a friendship with Mary in these missions after all. I give up. I do deserve to lose the one person that was close to me in my life." William, with despair as he walked further down the alley, heartbroken.

What Will didn't know was that Gabrielle watched him from the heavens and was angry at William for being selfish.

Four days past, Mary was at work charting down patient information with Elizabeth during their lunch break.

"Mary, you never told me? how your lunch went with William last Friday. So, how did it go?"

"The lunch went straight to the dirt, Elizabeth! During lunch, my fiance came to the restaurant unexpectedly saying that we had a lunch date to discuss the wedding plans for the final time. I introduced Matt to William and I could see in Matt's eyes that he hated Will after what he did to me back in high school, but Will apologized to me and Matt for what he did. While Matt and I were talking about the wedding plans, William got jealous of me getting married to another person that he got up and left the café! I couldn't believe that he did this to me! After that day, I didn't hear a word from Will!"

"Wow, what a friend Will is to you." Elizabeth, with shock after she heard Mary's story.

"I know and I think that he left Lake Park and went back to Sunnydale. Back to that Kathryn!" Mary spat out Kathryn's name.

"Don't say that Mare. Maybe William didn't leave town." Elizabeth closed the chart.

"I don't know about that Eliza. I don't know what I see in William anymore. What was I thinking, being his friend?"

CHAPTER EIGHT

A Saddened Decision

That evening, William was at home when Gabrielle appeared in a chair right next to him.

"How could you William? How could you easily let Mary see your selfishness come out when she told you that she was engaged? How can you let Mary go that easily and not give her another chance at friendship?"

"I wanted another chance at a love relationship with Mary, but she wouldn't, because she loves someone else. I don't think I'll be able to go through with these missions Gabrielle. I give up, I quit!" William told Gabrielle everything.

Gabrielle, looked at William with complete shock.

"How on earth can you say that William! How can you let the one person you love go when you know that you want her alive again? There are five missions in total involving with Mary's goals and dreams in her life. Right now in this mission, you are trying to win Mary back as your friend. Only in two missions, you will win Mary as your friend which is this mission and the Wife mission and only in three missions, you will win Mary back as your girlfriend which is the Teacher, Author, and Singer missions. I should've told you about the missions before I sent you on your first mission." Gabrielle blamed herself.

"You don't have to blame yourself Gabrielle. You were right, I was selfish and I was thought about myself. I have to win Mary back as my friend again and nothing else, but I don't know what to do now. I apologized to Mary twice and I don't even know if she'll forgive me this time." William apologized to Gabrielle.

"I'll give you some advice William. Why don't you call Mary tonight or tomorrow and apologize to her for what happened at the restaurant a few days ago. You should also tell Mary that you are happy for her that she's getting married."

"I don't know if I'll be able to say congratulations or I'm happy for you to Mary yet. I need sometime to think about my choice." William, unable to make a decision.

"Don't worry, I'll leave you sometime to think about your choice."

"Thank you Gabrielle for giving me another chance. I'll call you when I restore my friendship with Mary." William smiled.

"I'll be watching you William and good luck." Gabrielle disappeared in white smoke.

William took a phone book out from his desk drawer and looked up Mary's number. After a few minutes of looking, Will found Mary's number, went into the kitchen, picked up the phone, and called her.

"Hello." Mary answered the phone.

"Hey Mary, it's William."

"Why are you calling me?"

"I called you, because I want to apologize to you for what I did to you last week." Will told Mary his apology.

"Oh yeah apology the first minute and abandonment the next!" Mary drastically to William.

"No Mary. This time, my apology is real. I am really sorry for what happened last Friday at the coffee shop and I wanted to make it up to you by having lunch with you tomorrow if you aren't busy?"

"Are you really telling me the truth this time?" Mary doubted William.

"I am telling you the truth Mary. Now and forever more." Will told Mary.

"Okay, I believe you William and I will go out to lunch with you tomorrow since I have the day off tomorrow." Mary accepted Will's invitation.

"Great then. I'll see you tomorrow. I'll pick you up at twelve' thirty."

"See you then."

Wednesday, William picked up Mary exactly at twelve' thirty for lunch at Midtown Coffee Shop.

"So, what did you wanted to talk about?"

"I wanted to apologize to you for running out on you like that for nothing. You see, I was still upset after you told me that you are getting married to Matt. You know, I still have feelings for you."

"I understand Will. I knew you had feelings for me. I still have feelings for you too." Mary told William.

"Really, you do?"

"Yes, but I can connect you to Matt and Matt is just like you. I will always find you in Matt." Mary took William's hand that was on the table and held it.

"Mary... thank you for being there for me when I needed help." William smiled at Mary.

"I know, because you are my friend." Mary smiled back.

"You mean it, I am your friend again?"

"Yes, you are my best friend again Will, I can finally see that you came home and restored our relationship. You really do care about me."

"I'm your friend too Mary and I will always be around to protect you." William promised Mary.

An hour later, William and Mary left the café and walked back to Mary's apartment.

"Will, I am glad that you came home and repaired our friendship together." Mary hugged Will.

"I know and I am happy for coming back and filling the empty space that I had to fill in my heart. If it wasn't for your friend Susan telling me what happened to you, I wouldn't have fixed our friendship." William held onto Mary.

"Really? Susan told you everything?" Mary let go of William.

"Yes, she did."

"I guess I'm going to thank her the next time I talk to her. I'm glad that I helped you fill this space. Well, I'll talk to you later. I have to finish up with the wedding plans." Mary walked up to the apartment complex door.

"Yeah, I'll call you later." William walked home.

That evening, William was at his apartment when white smoke came from the chair.

"Hi Will, I wanted to check up on you and see if you made a decision. Did you see Mary today?"

"Yes I did and everything went well with Mary today. I also made a decision about your question last night."

"And, what is your decision? Did you repair your friendship with Mary, or go back to Sunnydale, back to Kathryn?"

"I decided to stay here in Lake Park with Mary and be her friend. I don't want to go back to Sunnydale. If I go back, I have nothing. I just want to be home in Lake Park and be there for Mary on her wedding day."

"Really, you decided to let Mary go as a girlfriend and let her be your friend?"

"Yes, I am letting Mary go as my girlfriend and just be her best friend like before we went out. I'm letting Mary be with Matt and marry him, because she loves him. I am finally moving on with my life and let Mary live her life with Matt."

"Will, I am proud of you. You are following your heart to do what's best for Mary and reuniting your fallen relationship with her. That's what I want you to do in these five missions, never give up. You can bring Mary back to life. You have to be strong, don't ever discourage yourself." Gabrielle happily to William.

"You're right Gaby. I can't give up. This is only the first mission, I need to focus on your orders and not focus on my thoughts. Sometimes, I may need to, but not all the time. There's only one thing that I have to say to Mary and I will tell her on Sunday."

"What are you going to tell Mary?"

"I'm going to tell Mary how happy I am for her and I want to be there on Mary's wedding day for her."

"That's wonderful! That's a perfect way to end your first mission William. A very good ending."

"I know it will." William smiled.

Saturday, Mary decided to go to William's apartment and surprise him.

"Hey William." Mary smiled at him.

"Hey Mare, what are you doing here?"

"I wanted to see you, because I wanted to tell you something."

"Sure, come in, come in." William let Mary into his apartment.

"You have a nice place William. It's really cozy." Mary walked into the living room and sat on the couch.

"Yeah, I'm still working on it though. I might not work on it anymore. It looks decent enough, but anyways, I like it." William brought a tray of coffee out to the living room.

"Cool." Mary took a cup of coffee from the tray.

"So, what did you wanted to tell me?"

"Well, I forgot to tell you yesterday that I wanted to invite you to the wedding on May seventeenth."

"You really want me to come to your wedding?"

"Yes, I want you to come. Besides, it wouldn't be much of a wedding if you weren't there." Mary begged William to come.

"Say no more Mary, I accept your invitation." William calmed Mary down.

"Thanks William! You are a great friend." Mary smiled.

"Mary, I wanted to say congratulations to you on your engagement to Matt. He's the perfect guy for you and I'm happy that you found that special someone in your life. I am letting you go to marry Matt, I'm ready to accept this, and move on with my life." William let Mary go.

"Oh William, thank you! I promise that this friendship won't be wasted this time." Mary happily hugged William.

"Hey, I was the one that screwed up our relationship Mary. I promise you that our friendship will be stronger than ever. I'll be here for you when you need help and when times go bad for you and Matt."

"Don't worry William. This friendship won't be wasted. You will be there for me no matter what happens to the both of us. Our friendship is special and it will never be broken." Mary hugged William again.

"I know it will Mary, I know." William held onto Mary.

Suddenly, Mary's body disappeared from William's arms and formed the shape of a spherical green orb.

"William, you did it! You completed your first mission!" Gabrielle appeared in the room.

"What?" William held the green orb in his hand.

"This means that you repaired the relationship with Mary as it was detained in each mission. Once you repaired your bond with Mary. She'll turn into an orb indicting that her dreams are in that orb along with the relationship with you. Like I said before to you." Gabrielle told Will about the orb.

"I can't believe it, I completed my first mission! Gabrielle, I am ready for the next mission!"

"As you wish, William." Gabrielle said as the apartment vanished leaving Gabrielle and William in a darkened state.

CHAPTER NINE

Mary, A Teacher

"William, are you sure that you are ready to go on your next mission?" Gabrielle, with concern.

"Yes, I am. I'm ready for my next mission." William, with dignity in his heart.

"Okay, if you are ready then let's go two years where Mary is twenty-five years old as an elementary school teacher." Gabrielle said as the scene shifted to an elementary school.

It was recess, children played and ran around the playground. William noticed a beautiful young woman helping a second grade girl who fell off the monkey bars.

"Gabrielle... Is that?" William pointed towards the teacher helping on the playground.

"Oh yes William. That is Mary Radcliffe as a first grade teacher at Shales Elementary school. The school that you and Mary went to when you both were kids." Gabrielle told William.

"Oh my god! Mary looks more beautiful and stunning just like how she was when she was still alive." William clung onto the fence.

"Will, do you want to know what happens to you and what you must do in this mission?"

"Yes, I want to know." William tore away from Mary and took Gabrielle's hand.

The scene changed from Lake Park, Illinois to Carson, Wisconsin in an apartment building.

"Gabrielle, where are we?" William looked around the apartment.

"William, you are in your hometown of Carson, Wisconsin. You see after you graduated high school, your parents got a call from your Aunt Jo in Wisconsin stating that your grandparents were very sick and suspected foul play for their illnesses. So, your parents took you back to Carson to take care of your grandparents. You never told your friends what was going on, but you did tell Mary about your grandparents." Gabrielle showed William a memory of him and Mary on their date at Langston Park.

"Mary, I need to tell you something." William quietly to his girlfriend as he held her hand.

"What is it?" Mary, with concern.

"Babe, I need to go back to Wisconsin for a while. My parents need my help to take care of my grandparents and get the people who are trying to kill my grandparents."

"No, you can't go! What about us? You are going to break up with me aren't you?" Mary panicked.

"No honey, listen to me. I'm not going to break up with you. What I'm saying is that we have to put our plans on hold. I promise to you babe that we will still be boyfriend and girlfriend. I will still talk to you, but this relationship will be a long distant one. When I come back, I will propose to you and we can start our lives together. I promise." William calmed Mary down.

"Okay Will, I believe you. I promise that I won't go with any other guys. I just want to be with you!" Mary fought back her tears and hugged her boyfriend.

"Don't worry Mary. I'll be back soon I promise." William held Mary in his arms as he kissed her hair and face.

The scene stopped and faded back to the apartment living room.

"After you left William, everyone thought you disappeared without a trace. Nine years later on this day, the people who tried to kill your grandparents came back and set the whole apartment on fire. You were the only one who survived the fire. Your mom Claire, your dad Ryan, your aunt Jo, your uncle Chris, your grandmother Sarah, and your grandmother Jack were all killed in the fire." Gabrielle told William the whole story.

"Oh my god, my family was murdered! By who?"

"They were murdered by your racist cousin Jessie and her racist gang, because she thinks that your family deceived her." Gabrielle told William the bad news.

There was a long pause from William. He couldn't believe that his own cousin killed his family for selfishness.

"What happens to Mary and I?" William sat down on the sofa.

"Well, after three years of waiting, Mary went to Northern Illinois University to major in teaching. Mary came back to Lake Park after graduation and she started teaching at her old elementary school as a first grade teacher. She works at Shales for two years now. You will be going to the hospital soon after this ordeal and I'll meet you at the hospital later. I'll tell you more about your mission when you get to hospital."

"Thanks Gaby. See you at the hospital."

"Come on William, help me get your grandmother out of the bedroom!" Claire got Sarah out of bed.

"Okay Mom!" William walked into the bedroom and helped his mom.

Suddenly, a crash came from the living room.

"What was that?" Sarah, with fright.

"Mom, look after Grandma. I'll go find out what happened in the living room." William told his mother and grandmother to stay put.

Will snuck into the living room to find his cousin Jessie with her Firedogs gang, Traci, Max, Terrell, and Mikayla.

"Jessie, please don't do this to us and your family! We care about you too much!" Chris begged.

"No Dad! You and Mom don't give a shit about me!" Jessie grabbed a shotgun out of her pocket and pointed it at Chris and Ryan.

William hid behind the couch and peered out from the top of the couch to see what was going on.

"Please Jessie, please put the gun down and listen to your father. He wants to help you and see you get better." Ryan tried to calm Jessie down.

"No, no, I won't go for help! I don't want to be locked up!" Jessie shouted.

"Jessie, please just listen to your uncle Ryan, please. It's for the best for you and our family." Chris grew closer to Jessie.

"I won't!" Jessie cried and fired gun shots.

Jessie shot her father three times in the chest and shot her uncle once in the head.

"Come on guys, the coast is clear. Help me kill the rest of my family!" Jessie stepped over her uncle's body and walked over to the kitchen.

William crawled out of his hiding spot and snuck towards Ryan.

"William, I need you to protect your mother, your grandparents, and your aunt. Just leave me. I tried to protect you and our family, but I failed." Ryan weakly.

"I promise Dad. I will protect our family for you." William cried.

"I am proud of you William, for not being like your cousin. Mary turned your life around and made you good. If you make this out alive, go back to Illinois, find Mary, and be with her. Can you promise me that William?"

"I will Dad. I promise I will go back to Lake Park, find Mary, and marry her. I won't let you down."

Ryan fell into unconsciousness afterwards.

"No, please Jessie, don't shoot! Please don't!" Jo screamed.

"Shut up Mother or else I will shoot!" Jessie threatened her mother and aunt.

"Please Jessie, don't do this to your family. We love you very much." Claire reassured her niece.

"No, you don't!" Jessie fired a bullet into Claire's chest.

Jessie walked over to Jo and shot her four times in the head.

Suddenly, shots fired from Jack and Sarah's room. William tip-toed towards the bedroom to find his mom and aunt dead.

"Jess, we took care of both your grandparents." Traci came out of the bedroom.

"Good. Now, let's torch the place!" Jessie walked down the hall.

William crawled underneath the kitchen table as the Firedogs walked into the kitchen.

Traci turned on the stove, but before Jessie could light the stove, there was a loud noise.

"What was that?"

"It came from underneath that table!" Mikayla pointed to the table.

"Let's see what's underneath the table." Jessie loaded her gun.

Mikayla lifted the tablecloth to reveal William.

"I should've known that my cousin would betray me and call the police on me! Grab him Mikayla!" Jessie looked at William with disgust.

Mikayla dragged Will out from underneath the table as Max and Terrell walked into the kitchen.

"Well William, you tried to turn me in, but now you face the consequences!" Jessie looked at her cousin with an angry look on her face.

"Jessie, please don't hurt me! I'll keep your secret and I won't turn you in!" William begged Jessie.

"Max, Terrell, take care of my cousin. I had enough of his lies! I'll take the final blow when I'm ready."

After five minutes of Terrell and Max beating Will, Jessie walked up to her cousin who moaned on the floor.

"I'm sorry to do this Will, but this is the way it gotta be." Jessie pointed the gun at William's face and fired it.

The bullet grazed Will's head and hit the floor. William passed out after the bullet hit the floor.

"Come on guys, show's over. Terrell, torch the place!" Jessie walked out of the kitchen with her gang.

Terrell took a box of matches out of his pocket, lit one, and threw it onto the gassed stove.

The stove exploded and the kitchen was on fire. Papers that led from the other rooms to the stove were on fire.

William woke up to the smell of gas. It was too late to save his family so, William ran to the front door. The flames caught up as Will ran into the third floor hallway.

The hallway was packed with people evacuating the building that William jumped out the third floor window. He landed on the pavement outside as people ran across the street to safety. William fell into unconsciousness as the sirens of the fire trucks, police, and the paramedics arrived at the scene.

The next thing William knew was that he was at Lukarton Medical Center. He was in room 207 with cuts, bruises, and minor burns on his body.

"Gabrielle, where are you?" William looked around the room.

"I'm right here Will as promised." Gabrielle sat next to William.

"I couldn't believe that my own cousin killed my own family! I can't believe it! What's going to happen to me now?" Will cried.

"Isn't it obvious William. You have to contact Mary and get back together with her. You know, she is single and she thinks that you will come back to her and things will be right again." Gabrielle advised William.

"You're right Gaby. I don't belong here in my hometown anymore. I belong with Mary back in Lake Park."

"Once after you settle things with the police and your family's funerals, you go back to Illinois and win Mary back." Gabrielle disappeared.

There was a knock at the door, a Nurse's Assistant came into the room with a police officer and a detective.

"William, there's a detective that wants to question you about the apartment fire that happened today."

"Hello Mr. Valmont, I am Detective David Carlson from the Carson Police Department. I want to ask you a couple of questions about today's fire at Ridge Hill apartment complex." Detective Carlson introduced himself to William.

"Okay."

"Now, can you tell me what happened before the fire began." Detective Carlson sat next to Will.

"Well, I was helping my mother, Claire move my grandmother, Sarah out of the apartment after my aunt Jo and my uncle Chris received a threatening letter from my cousin Jessie."

Why was your cousin threatening your family?"

"She's deranged! She thinks that we don't love her anymore and she turned racist after she graduated from high school. One day she got into a fight with her parents that she ran away from home. Jessie joined a gang called the Firedogs and she wanted revenge on my family for betraying her that she made my grandfather, Jack and my grandmother, Sarah sick."

"Okay and did you see your cousin when the fire happened today?" Detective Carlson wrote down the information.

"Yes, she was the one that started the fire! Before she set the fire, Jessie and her gang shot every one of my family members to death. She shot me, but the bullet grazed my head and hit the floor which made me pass out. When I came to, I saw the apartment in flames. I couldn't save my family, so I had to get out of the building. The third floor hallway was so jammed that I had to jump out the window."

"Okay Mr. Valmont. We'll look for your cousin, the Firedogs, and take them into custody. I want you to rest and we'll tell you when we catch your cousin." Detective Carlson wrote down the last bit of information and left the hospital room.

Meanwhile in Lake Park, Mary read, Clara's Pet Business to her class during story time.

"What did you think of the story children?" Mary closed the book.

"I liked the part with all the pets that Clara had to take care of." Kyla Patrick smiled.

"That was the best book you read to us, Ms. Radcliffe!" Zachary Smith, happily to his teacher.

"That gives me an idea for Art time. I would like all of you to draw a picture of your favorite animal that you would like to have in your life. After Art time, you all can present your pictures to the class."

Later on, Mary looked at the clock and it was around two' forty-five.

"All right class, let's present your drawings before we go home. Anne, why don't you start first?"

"Ms. Radcliffe, I drew a dolphin, because they are silly, they splash water around, and they are fun to be around." Anne Jenkins presented her picture.

"Very good Anne! An excellent drawing. Um Alec, why don't you go next?"

"I drew a tiger, because tigers are my favorite animal and I would like to have a tiger someday." Alec Somerset presented his project.

"Excellent drawing Alec. Maybe you will get your tiger someday or even be a tiger tamer. Tara, why don't you go next?"

"I drew a seal, because I love water animals and one day, I would like to live with the seals." Tara Mitchell presented.

As Tara presented her animal, Mary thought about her perfect life.

My dream has finally come true. I can't believe I'm an elementary school teacher, teaching at my old elementary school. I love my students and I'm an excellent teacher. I have a perfect life. What can ruin this moment in my life!

"Ms. Radcliffe, it's almost time to go home." Viola Hart looked at the clock.

"You're right Viola. Everyone hand in your pictures and don't forget to do pages 30 and 31 in your math workbook and pages 26 and 27 in your writing workbooks. We'll go over them on Monday! Have a great weekend class."

"Bye Ms. Radcliffe!"

Later on in the Teacher's Lounge, Mary graded papers and had a cup of coffee. Mary went back to the coffee machine and filled her cup up. There was a milk spill on the floor. Mary walked into the spill, slipped and fell to the floor, bringing her coffee, sugar container, and the salt container with her. George Creedson, who just walked into the lounge noticed Mary's fall.

"Hey, are you all right?" George helped Mary up.

"Oh yes, I'm all right. Oh man, I spilled everything on the floor!" Mary noticed the mess on the floor.

Here, let me help you clean this mess." George walked over to the sink and grabbed a few paper towels.

"Thanks. I'm Mary Radcliffe. I teach first grade." Mary introduced herself to George as she took the towels from him.

"I'm George Creedson. I teach fourth grade." George introduced himself to Mary.

"Hey, I've seen you at assemblies and yesterday when you helped me with that second grader." Mary recognized George.

"Yes and I've seen you at the office and during recess duty. You know, you are a great teacher to the students here at this school." George took the paper towels from Mary.

CHAPTER TEN

An Unexpected Person

On Monday, Mary had recess duty and so did George.
"Hey Mary." George walked up to Mary.

"Hey George, how was your weekend?"

"The weekend was all right. I had to tutor one of my students who was having trouble in math. How was your weekend?" George told Mary about his weekend.

"It was pretty good. My sister Kaylin gave birth to a baby boy. She named him after her husband, Steve and he is so cute and adorable!"

"Tell your sister that I said congratulations to her for me." George, happily to Mary.

"I will George. Tonight, Kaylin is coming home from the hospital so I'm going to help her with the baby while Steve is out of town on business. Who's the student that you needed to tutor in math?"

"Oh, her name is Sarah Gregson and she's in my class. You see, I'm running homework club for all the grades in this school."

"Nice. Um, do you need any help for homework club? Do you need more teachers to help the students?"

"Not right now, but you can come and check the club out. If your students need any help in class, maybe I can help them."

"Sure, I'll do that." Mary smiled.

"Great. Well, I better get back and patrol the playground with the other teachers. I'll see you after school in the lounge?"

"Yeah, I'll see you in the lounge after school and I promise that I won't spill anything this time."

"I hope not and besides, you had an off day Mary. Everyone has their off days sometimes. I'll see you at 2:40 then." George looked at Mary and walked away.

"See you later." Mary watched George walk back to the playground.

Meanwhile, back in Wisconsin, William was released from the hospital and was at a nearby friend's house.

"I can't believe that your own cousin started that fire last week and killed your family! Did the police ever catch Jessie and her gang?" Justin Clearbolt with shock at William.

"I talked to the police before I left the hospital. They told me that they caught them who were running from the apartment complexes. The Firedogs and Jessie were arrested and charged with the murders of my family members. I can't focus on the funerals or even stay here anymore, because its too painful to be here in Wisconsin! I have to get out of here!" William panicked.

"You should get out of here Will. You should go back to Lake Park, Illinois and find that girl you dated. What was her name?"

"Mary Radcliffe." William softly answered Justin's question.

"Yeah, that was her name. Mary was such a nice girl. I don't know why you left her Will. I bet she misses you and probably still waiting for you to come back to her."

"Yes, Mary does miss me. I wonder if she's thinking about me and hasn't moved on in her life without me?" William sighed about Mary.

"Why don't you call her and tell her that you want to go back to her. Do you have her number?" Justin advised William to reconnect with Mary again.

"I still have her home phone number, but I don't know if she's still living at home anymore."

"Well go on, call her!" Justin picked up the phone and gave it to William.

"All right, I will." William took the phone from Justin.

"I'll leave you alone to talk to her." Justin left the room.

William dialed the number and waited for someone to answer.

"Hello?" A woman answered the phone.

"Hi Mrs. Radcliffe, this is William Valmont. Is Mary there?"

"Oh William, I'm sorry, but Mary doesn't live here at home anymore."

"What! Where is she living at now?" William with shock.

"Mary is still here in Lake Park, but at the Shady Lane apartment complexes off of Princeton Road." Petra answered William's question.

"Okay. Can I have her number so I can call her?"

"Sure. It's (877)-249-7831." Petra gave the number to Will.

"Thank you Mrs. Radcliffe. I'll give Mary a call right now. It was nice talking to you again." William wrote down the number.

"No problem William. It was nice talking to you again too. Take care of yourself. Bye." Petra hung up.

After school, Mary was in the Teacher's Lounge with George while they had coffee.

"So Mare, how was class today?" George brought Mary a fresh cup of coffee.

"It was great. I took my students outside for twenty minutes before the bell rang for dismissal. We also finished up our animal presentations and the students did an excellent job drawing their animals that before I go home, I'm going to hang up the pictures on the wall next to my classroom. How about you? How was your day?"

"Well, I had to send one of my students to the office, because he was disturbing the class, but afterwards the day was all right for me."

"It looks like you had a bad day George. Hey, don't worry about that student. Just forget about today and think about tomorrow. Here, take this." Mary hugged George, and gave him a small piece of paper.

George opened the paper revealing Mary's cell number written on the paper.

"You can call me anytime when you have any problems of if you just want to talk." Mary looked at George.

"Thanks Mary, you always find a way to make me smile and make me feel better about myself." George cheered up.

"That's what people do for other people that they care about." Mary smiled.

The next thing Mary knew was that George kissed her straight on her lips until Mary's cell phone went off in her pocket.

"Uh-oh, my sister is texting me. I better call Kaylin and tell her that I'll be late. I better get going. I'll see you tomorrow George." Mary looked at her phone.

"All right. Tell your sister that I said hi. I'll see you tomorrow Mary." George kissed Mary's cheek and walked away.

That evening around eight' thirty, Mary graded papers and put together tomorrow's lesson when her cell phone rang.

"Hello?" Mary answered her phone.

"Hi Mary, this is William Valmont."

"William… is it really you?" Mary dropped her pen onto the floor.

"Yes it's me Mary. How are you these days?"

"Well after we lost contact in July of 2012, I went to school and became an elementary school teacher. I teach first grade and I got a teaching job at our old elementary school. How's it going with your family? Are those people still after your family?"

"Well, four days ago, my cousin Jessie and her gang came to my grandparent's apartment and murdered my family! After she shot me, she set the apartment on fire! Mary, I've been released from the hospital a few days ago and I don't want to be here in Wisconsin anymore. I want to come back to Illinois, back to you!" William cried and begged to come home.

"Okay William, calm down. If you want to come home, then come home. Are you still in Carson, Wisconsin?"

"Yes, I am still. I'm staying with Justin Clearbolt, an old friend of mine until tomorrow. I'm taking the two' thirty flight from Wisconsin to Illinois."

"Well, you can stay with me until you can get on your feet again." Mary invited William to come and stay with her.

"You will?"

"Yes. I'll do anything for a friend." Mary kept her promise.

"Thank you Mary. I will be in Lake Park around three' forty-five in the afternoon." William told Mary.

"Okay. I'll get out of work right away after school ends, pick you up at O' Hare Airport, and bring you to my apartment to settle in." Mary told William the plan for tomorrow.

"Okay. I'll see you tomorrow then."

Tuesday, Mary was at work teaching her students how to write the letters from the alphabet in cursive starting from I through R.

"All right class, I want you all to practice drawing Q. I will help you if you have any trouble writing out the letter." Mary wrote on the chalkboard.

During recess, Mary ate lunch in the lounge and thought about William. She was reminiscing the day that William took her to meet his family.

It was the summer of 2007 on the fourth of July weekend, William invited Mary to meet his whole family at a barbeque at his house.

"Mary, I would like you to meet my Aunt Jo, Uncle Chris, and my little cousin Jessie." William introduced Mary to his relatives.

"It's so nice to meet you all. William has told me a lot about you." Mary smiled, hugged Jo, shook Chris's hand, and hugged Jessie.

"William told wonderful things about you Mary. It's nice to finally meet you!" Jo happily hugged Mary again.

"Ryan has told us how you helped our nephew get back on the right track and bringing our family together again all thanks to you Mary." Chris patted Mary's shoulder and hugged her.

"Yeah, woo-hoo!" Jessie gave Mary dirty looks and not caring.

Mary looked at Jessie in shock and went to William's side.

"I can't believe that Will's cousin did this to him and murdered her own family! I never did trust Jessie at all after we first met each other. She was deranged and always mean to her family and me."

By the time school ended, Mary went to the lounge to get her things and head to O' Hare airport. She was about to walk out the door when she bumped into George.

"Hi Mary, where are you going in such a hurry?"

"I'm sorry George, but I can't talk to you right now. I have to go pick up an old friend of mine at the airport in Chicago." Mary walked out the door.

"Okay, I'll call you later tonight."

Mary didn't pay attention to George as she left the school.

At O' Hare Airport, Mary waited at gate 13-B for William's plane to arrive. Mary, nervous to see the man she loved ever since seventh grade and helped him throughout their high school years.

"May I have your attention please, United Airlines flight 172 from Green Bay to Chicago has just landed."

A couple of minutes later, Mary noticed a man with light-brown hair, blue eyes, and wearing glasses. William recognized a woman with chocolate-brown hair and brown eyes that he ran up to her. They both looked at each other for a couple of seconds and they rushed into each other's arms.

"Oh Mary, its been so long since we've seen each other." William cried as he held onto Mary.

"It's so good to see you again." Mary smiled happily as she stroked William's hair.

"You changed a lot since the last time I saw you."

"I missed you so much. I thought I was never going to see you again." Mary looked into Will's eyes.

"I missed you too Mare. I am so glad that I am back home in Illinois." William smiled.

"I'm glad you are home again. Come on, let's go get your things and head to Lake Park." Mary walked towards baggage claim.

At Mary's apartment half an hour later, Mary showed William her place.

"And this is your room. I hope you'll like staying in this room."

"Don't worry Mare, I like this room." William smiled.

"Great. Here, I'll let you unpack while I get dinner started." Mary smiled as she walked out of the room.

As Will unpacked his things, he was happy that he made the right choice to come home and repair his relationship with Mary.

"Hey, how's it going?" Mary knocked on the door.

"Huh, oh yes, I'm already unpacked." William put his suitcase under the bed.

"That's great, because dinner is almost ready."

"Okay, I'll be in the kitchen in a couple of minutes." William hugged Mary.

"Hey, it's no problem. I do anything for an old friend." Mary held onto William.

"So Will, why did your cousin murdered your family?" Mary poured macaroni onto his plate.

"Well, we received a threatening letter from Jessie two weeks ago. By Friday, Jessie ambushed us. I was helping my mom with my grandmother trying to get her out of the apartment when we heard a loud crash. I told my mom to stay with my grandmother while I went to investigate the crash. I snuck into the living room to find my dad, my uncle Chris, and Jessie arguing about her and the family. I hid behind the couch until I heard gun shots. After Jessie and her gang walked into the hallway, I walked over to my dad on the floor in a pool of blood, dying. He told me to leave him and save the rest of my family. He died soon afterwards. I heard more shots and I knew that the rest of my family members were dead. I had to save myself and get out of the apartment fast. I heard footsteps that I ran into the kitchen and hid underneath the table. I heard the Firedogs coming into the kitchen saying that they killed everyone. Before they torched the apartment, I accidentally hit my head on the table. They heard me, dragged me from the table, they beat me up until Jessie shot me near my head. The next thing I knew, I woke up to find the place on fire. As I ran to the exit, the flames followed me until I got into a jam packed hallway. I couldn't get out so I jumped out of a window."

"Oh my god. I can't believe your own cousin murdered your family! I'm so glad that you weren't seriously injured or even worse!" Mary cried.

"Mary, don't worry about what happened to me in Wisconsin. I am okay. I'm not hurt anymore. I am very lucky to be alive and to be here with you." William got up from his chair, walked over to Mary, and consoled her.

"I know that you are here, but I don't want to see or hear about you getting hurt again. I couldn't bear to see you dead or hurt!" Mary cried as William held her in his arms and stroked her hair.

"Don't worry Mary, I'm not going anywhere. I am staying by your side and never leaving you again." William promised Mary that he would always stay with her no matter what happens.

CHAPTER ELEVEN

A Secret Crush

Later on that evening, white swirls with golden sparkle smoke filled the room and Gabrielle appeared from the smoke.

"Hi William. I see that you are back in Lake Park." Gabrielle sat on the bed.

"Yes, I am glad to be back home and back with Mary. I can't wait to rekindle our relationship again."

"Um William, there is something that I need to tell you. While you were in Wisconsin trying to get out, I observed Mary and she met this man named George Creedson. He teaches fourth grade at the same school where she works at and he has a crush on Mary."

"What?"

"It's true William. Mary has also developed a crush on George Creedson."

"I have to prevent this guy from asking the girl I love to be his girlfriend! I need to take drastic measures to win Mary's heart again!" William panicked.

"Then I suggest you make your move before George does." Gabrielle advised William.

"I will Gabrielle. I lost my family and I lost Mary once, I am not going to lose her again! I don't want Mary to end up with someone who will treat her bad and won't love her for the rest of her life." William fell into his desk chair into depression.

"I'll leave you alone to make your decision and I'll come back in a few days to check on you." Don't worry William, you'll win Mary back, you'll see." Gabrielle patted William's shoulder and disappeared from the room.

William sat in the chair for several minutes as he sank into thoughts of Mary enjoying a life with George and being happy with him instead of living a life with William.

"That's it! I am going to repair my loveship with Mary right now! Whether she takes me back or not!" William angrily snapped out of the visions in his head.

William walked out of his room, went to Mary's bedroom, and knocked on the door.

"Come in." Mary packed her bag for tomorrow.

"Mary, can I tell you something?" William closed the door.

"Sure William. What is it that you wanted to tell me?" Mary sat on the bed.

"Mary, I know you are mad at me for leaving you alone without me to take care of you. I wanted to see you so badly over the past eight years, even though we were going through a long-distant relationship and we drifted away. I never cheated on you while I was away. You can blame me for letting this all happen and I regret it for leaving you. All I know is that I want another chance to be your boyfriend and I want you to be my girlfriend again." William begged and grasped Mary's hand.

"Oh William… I can't say yes to you right now, because there's another guy that I like right now."

"Are you going to go with that guy and be his girlfriend?" William with sorrow.

"I don't know yet William. I still need to make my decision." Mary, undecided.

A few hours later around eleven, William couldn't sleep. He had bad dreams of what happened a few hours ago and Mary's future. William had to do something to change Mary's mind from choosing George and to choose him. Ideas swirled into William's head as the words combined into a song. William looked at his guitar next to his desk, picked it up, and left the room.

"Mary, you are the sweetest girl in the world.
You brightened up my life.
You gave me strength.
You were even there for me when I was down.

I don't want to lose you now.
I know what I did was wrong.
I don't want to lose you now.
Let me have a second chance to prove myself to you.

You gave me faith.
You gave me life.
All I know is that I love you.
All I want to do is be here for you and love you until the end of time." William sang into Mary's darkened room.

Mary awoke from her sleep to hear singing outside her window. She put on her red robe, red flip-flops, and walked over to the window. Mary found William in the yard singing a love song to her and only her. She walked onto the balcony and watched William sing.

"I won't abandon you.
I won't desert you.
I won't cheat on you.
I don't want to fall in love with any other girl.
All I want, is to fall in love with you and only you.
You mean the world to me and I would do anything for you.
Please Mary, take me back and I promise you that I'll never leave your side again." William finished up his song.

"Oh William, that was a beautiful song." Mary smiled and cried a little as she clapped her hands.

"This song is for you Mary and I wrote it for you tonight. I wanted to tell you how much I love you how much I love you before you make your decision." William climbed the balcony and sat next to Mary.

"I am so sorry for telling you that George Creedson wanted to ask me out. You must be in so much stress about this." Mary hugged William

"It has been a lot of stress on me Mary, ever since you told me after dinner tonight. All I know is that I love you and I want to be with you… just you! Will you please, please go out with me again?" William begged Mary.

Mary thought about Will's question a lot and the song that he sang for her. She fell hard in love with William when he sang the song to her. Mary didn't want to lose him from her life if she didn't accept his offer.

"Yes, I will go out with you." Mary accepted William's plea.

"Really, you mean it?"

"Yes. You finally made me realize that you are the only person that I love in my life. I love you William Valmont." Mary placed her hand on William's face and kissed him.

As Mary kissed William, he felt that he just completed the mission, but there was something else that he needed to complete it.

Wednesday, Mary packed her things before she went to work.

"Hey babe, have a great day at work all right." William held Mary and kissed her cheek.

"I will. Good luck with the job searching hon." Mary touched Will's face.

"Don't worry, I will find a job and besides, there's an opening for a photographer's position at the Lake Park Journal. I'll get the job and support you and our home."

"Don't worry about supporting me Will. Just focus on the job and impressing the boss. I'll see you at four." Mary calmed her boyfriend down and she grabbed her bag.

"Yes, I'll see you later." William smiled at his girl.

At Shales elementary fifteen minutes later, Mary was in her classroom going through her lesson plan and grading tests before class began.

"Hello Mary." George knocked on the door and walked into the classroom.

"Oh hi George. How's it going?" Mary looked up at George and smiled at him.

"Hey, I was thinking tomorrow night, I was going to take you to A Midsummer's Dream at the Shakespeare Theater at Navy Pier and afterwards, I'll take you around the lake on a boat." George told Mary that he wanted to take her on a date.

"Um George… listen… I can't go out with you tomorrow, because I have a date with someone else." Mary turned George down.

""Oh, it's okay, it's okay, I understand. Hey, I'll see you around." George left the classroom.

Mary knew that she hurt George and she had to make it up to him.

Recess later on, Mary was on recess duty while she looked for George, but she couldn't find him.

"Hey Natalie, does George have recess duty today?"

"Oh Mary, he doesn't have recess duty today. He has recess duty tomorrow." Natalie answered Mary's question.

"Oh thanks Nat." Mary, with disappointment.

"Mary! Mary!" A voice called out to Mary.

Mary turned around to find William standing over by the fence shouting for her.

"Mary, is that your old boyfriend, William Valmont?" Natalie looked at William.

"Yes, he came back yesterday and we got back together. I wonder what's he doing here. Will, what are you doing here?" Mary asked in shock as she ran out of the school yard and into her boyfriend's arms.

"I wanted to come see you Mary, because I got the photography job!"

"Oh my god, congratulations!" Mary, happily kissed Will.

That evening while William put the rest of his things away in Mary's room while white smoke began to fill the room to reveal Gabrielle.

"Hi William, I wanted to see your progress so far on the mission. How's everything going?" Gabrielle looked around the room.

"Everything is perfect Gabrielle! I won Mary's heart and I got a job as a photographer at the Lake Park Journal newspaper!"

"How did you win Mary's heart?"

"Right after you left and after Mary turned me down, I thought of ideas for a song, wrote them down, I grabbed my guitar, and sang the song for Mary outside her bedroom window."

"Oh William, I am so happy and so proud of you. You got the love of your life back! When are you going to take Mary out on a date?"

"I'm taking Mary out tomorrow after she gets home from work. I am going to take her to Langston Park for a boat ride across the lake, after that, I'm taking her to this new restaurant that just opened called, The Shooting Star for a romantic dinner for two and afterwards, we are going for a night out in the city."

"Oh, Mary will be swept off her feet by the end of the night tomorrow." Gabrielle smiled.

"I know and before the night ends tomorrow, I'm going to tell Mary that I'm going to make a full-time commitment to her." William told Gabrielle.

"Oh William, you are so noble to do this for Mary. You are doing so well in this mission that soon you will be on the next mission. I'll let you continue your life with Mary and I'll come back within a couple of months. I might just bring a surprise for you to give to Mary." Gabrielle disappeared.

"What does she mean by a surprise?"

"Hey hon, dinner will be ready soon. Are you settled in?" Mary walked into the room.

"Yeah, I am settled in. Can't wait for tomorrow, Mare?" William put his arms around Mary and held her.

"I can't wait for tomorrow either Will! It'll be just like the old days when you used to take me out on dates." Mary touched William's face and gazed into his eyes.

Will looked into Mary's eyes for a couple of minutes and kissed her.

Friday afternoon at Shales, Mary helped Fernando Alvarado with his flower that he made for his mom on Mother's Day during Art time when William walked into the classroom.

"William, what are you doing here?" Mary put down the rose and walked up to her boyfriend.

"Mary, I couldn't wait for you to come home from work so I can take you on our date. So I decided to take you from school and go on our date right now." William looked at Mary.

"Okay, but first I want to introduce you to my students before I get Natalie." Mary looked at William.

"Okay, you don't have to rush." William touched Mary's shoulder.

"Everyone, put down your things for a couple of minutes. I want to introduce you all to a special someone. This is William Valmont, my boyfriend. William, these are my special students that I teach everyday."

"It is nice to meet you all." William waved.

"Students, for the rest of the day, you'll have Ms. Bakerton as your substitute teacher. I expect you all to be on your best behavior. You can continue working on your art projects or work on your homework assignments that are on the board for the weekend." Mary told her students as Natalie walked into the classroom with her students.

"Thanks for watching my class Natalie. I appreciate it."

"No problem Mare. What are friends for. Have a great time with Will tonight." Natalie told her friend.

"I will. See you." Mary walked out the door with William.

At Langston Park, William placed a blindfold over Mary's eyes and surprise her.

"Will, what's the surprise? You can tell me. I'll still be surprised." Mary with excitement as William helped her out of the car.

"I can't tell you. I'll take the blindfold off when we get to the place where I'm taking you." William took Mary's hand and led her to the lake.

William took Mary to a dock and took off the blindfold.

"Oh my god, is this where you are taking me?" Mary looked at a boat alongside the lake.

"Yes it is. I'm taking you on a boat ride along the lake." William helped Mary onto the boat.

"This is so romantic William. I've always wanted to go on a boat ride along this lake!" Mary, with excitement.

"Mary, may I have this dance?" William held out his hand to Mary as the music played.

"Yes, you may." Mary smiled, took William's hand, and walked over to the dance floor.

"Will, this has been the best date I ever had in my life." Mary smiled as William held her in his arms as they danced.

"I want you to have a great time with me tonight, because you are special to me." William lifted Mary's chin and looked into her eyes.

"You are the best boyfriend I ever had." Mary laid her head on Will's shoulder.

"I know and I'm happy to be with you." William stroked Mary's hair.

Around five' thirty, the boat ride was over and William took his girl to the Shooting Star restaurant downtown.

"William, this has been the most wonderful night I had in my entire life." Mary walked across the bridge.

"I'm glad that you had a great night Mary. I wanted to celebrate us coming back together." William held Mary.

"I'm so glad we are back together. I thought you'd never come back to Lake Park, I thought you disappeared forever." Mary held onto her boyfriend.

"It's okay hon. I am here now for you. I am never leaving you again. Listen, there is something I need to tell you." William looked at Mary.

"What is it?"

"Mary...I... I..." William tried to get the words out of his mouth.

"Yes, tell me Will."

"Mary, I... I... I want to make a full-time commitment to you!" William spilled the words out of his mouth.

"What?" Mary, with shock.

"Yes, I want to make a full-time commitment to you and only you. When I came back to Lake Park and you helped me get back on my feet, I knew that you were the only girl for me and I want to be here for you always. Mary, I want to be your boyfriend, yours and forever more."

"Oh William, I will be your girlfriend now and forever more." Mary touched Will's face.

CHAPTER TWELVE

The Proposal

It was fall in Lake Park, Mary taught new first graders for another year. William got promoted to Entertainment Reporter for the Lake Park Journal. They were near their sixth month anniversary when Gabrielle paid William a surprise visit while Will wrote an article for the paper that night.

"Hi Gabrielle, come to check on my progress?" William put his laptop on the table.

"Yes, I saw your date with Mary and making a full-time commitment to her and I thought that was the sweetest thing you ever done for her. You are doing an excellent job in this mission that I wanted to give you something to give to Mary." Gabrielle pulled out a silver box from her white dress.

"What's that?"

"Here, open it." Gabrielle handed the silver box to William.

William opened the box to find a diamond silver ring.

"Gabrielle, is this a ..." William took out the ring.

"Yes William, that is an engagement ring and I want you to propose to Mary. You see, you're getting your chance to ask Mary to marry you before all this mess happened. This is the only mission that you'll propose to Mary. I'll give you sometime to think about it and I'll leave you the ring. I'll come back as soon as you make your decision." Gabrielle disappeared.

William looked at the diamond ring for a couple of minutes and knew that he had to propose to Mary. There was no trouble and Felicia wasn't around to cause trouble. Everything was perfect and he was happy with Mary. He put the ring back into the box and placed it into his desk drawer.

Two days went by and William thought about the proposal. He thought about how Mary died in the car crash and her funeral before he went on these missions.

"I know Mary doesn't know about the unmeaning affair with Felicia and she isn't here to stop me from proposing to Mary. I know that I made so many mistakes in my life and Mary helped me through it all. I'm going to make the right decision and I don't want to lose Mary again. I'm going to ask Mary to marry me and no one is going to stop me!"

Later on, Mary came home from work that same day, she was upset.

"Hi honey, how was your day?" William walked up to his girlfriend, hugged her, and kissed her.

"Oh school was okay except for one of my students. He wouldn't listen or do any of his work. So, I sent him to the Principal's Office. For the rest of my day, it was pretty good." Mary told her boyfriend her day.

"Oh, I'm sorry that you had a bad day. Is there anything I can do for you?"

"I just need to be with you tonight. You always make me smile whenever I have a bad day." Mary looked at her boyfriend.

"All right, we'll stay in tonight and watch movies together. I won't go to work tonight. I'll stay home with you." William held Mary's hands.

"Thanks Will, you are the best." Mary kissed William.

"Okay Mary, you go change while I make dinner for the both of us." William walked into the kitchen.

Mary changed into a pink t-shirt with black pajama pants. When she came into the dining room, she found the table set for two with candles all around. William walked out of the kitchen with two covered plates.

"Hey honey, you look very lovely tonight." William placed the plates on the table and kissed Mary's cheek.

"Stop it Will! I'm in my pajamas, I'm not lovely!" Mary blushed and sat down.

William chuckled and he took the covers off the plates.

"Babe, dinner looks delicious. What are we having?" Mary looked at her plate.

"It's your favorite pasta Mary, chicken parmesan. Remember our first date when we were in high school, we went to the Vines of the Vineyard. You ordered the chicken parmesan dish and you said to me that chicken parmesan was your favorite pasta dish. So, I decided to make it for dinner tonight." William sat at the table.

"Oh, that is the sweetest thing you've done for me. I haven't had chicken parmesan in a long time." Mary smiled and ate.

"Honey, since you did the cooking tonight, I volunteer to do the dishes." Mary laid next to William on the bed.

"No sweetheart. Today is your day to relax. I'll do the dishes tomorrow before I go to work." William held Mary in his arms.

"Okay." Mary set her head on her boyfriend's lap.

During the movie, William stroked Mary's hair, kissed her, and held her. Mary felt cheerful to spend time with her boyfriend. Usually, she would spend her nights alone since Will works afternoons and nights at the newspaper. Tonight, he would be there for her for comfort.

"Are you feeling better now that I'm here?" William held his girl in bed.

"Yes, I feel so much better. You know, I am glad that I didn't move on with my life without you. Otherwise, things wouldn't have happened like this if you stayed in Wisconsin." Mary touched William's face and looked into his eyes.

"I know. You would be sad and depressed without me with you. I am keeping my promise and my commitment to never leave you again." William held and kissed Mary's hand.

Wednesday morning, Mary went to work while William washed the breakfast and dinner dishes in the kitchen.

"Gabrielle, I need to talk to you about my proposal to Mary."

"So William, what did you want to talk to me about?"

"Gaby, I made my decision about Mary and I am going to propose to her." William sat at the table with Gabrielle.

"That's wonderful William! I am so proud of you for making the right decision to marry your girlfriend. When are you going to propose to her?"

"I don't know exactly when I'll propose to her, but it will be at a special place on a special day. Just like how I was going to propose to Mary on her birthday before all this happened." William described the proposal date to Gabrielle.

"We'll make it special for Mary okay. I'll let you think about the day you will propose to Mary. I'll be watching everything until you finish up your mission." Gabrielle disappeared from the table.

"The perfect day to propose to Mary, but when?"

Two months past and it was three days before Christmas Eve. Mary was on Christmas break from school. Will had to decide about the day he was going to propose to Mary. He couldn't wait forever to ask her.

Tuesday around four in the morning, William woke up nauseous. He got out of bed and quickly ran into the bathroom. Will puked into the toilet for a short time. He had another nightmare about Mary again. This was the seventh nightmare he had since the end of November. William dreamt that he secretly got back together with Felicia while he dated Mary.

Mary came home from work to find clothes scattered around the living room and in the hallway.

"Will, are you here?" Mary looked at the clothes puzzled.

Mary opened the bedroom door to find William making love to Felicia in their bed.

"What the hell is this? William, what are you doing with this slut?" Mary exclaimed.

"Mary, this isn't what you think." William got out of bed.

"Yeah, you are cheating on me with another girl! I gave you everything that I could ever give you, but you went behind my back and went with another girl! I'm through with you... forever!" Mary with anger as she left the room.

"Mary... wait!" William grabbed some clothes from his dresser and ran after Mary.

Mary was in her car and halfway out of the parking lot when William got into his car. Mary headed out of Lake Park on route 31, going to Hillcrest, and into South Hollow Wood. Mary stopped in the middle of an intersection and realized that William followed her.

Before Will could get out of his car to straighten things out with Mary, her car was hit by another car, carried her to a tree, and exploded.

William shook himself out of his memories, flushed the toilet, and sat on the floor. He was stressed out from the dreams he's been having about Mary that he couldn't concentrate on planning his proposal to Mary. He started to cry, because he started to have second thoughts on his proposal.

Meanwhile, Mary turned and woke up to find William gone. Mary got up and walked into the hallway. She noticed light from the bathroom.

"William, honey, are you in there?" Mary knocked on the door.

"Huh? Oh yeah, I'm in here." William sat on the floor.

"Are you all right? Can I come in?"

"No, because I'm coming out." William got up and opened the door.

Mary noticed that Will was crying and upset about something.

"Will, come here. Why don't we sit in the living room and talk about what's really bothering you." Mary looked and touched her boyfriend.

"Okay."

In the living room, Will sat on the couch as Mary turned on the light and sat next to him.

"Now tell me, what is upsetting you." Mary held William's hand.

William couldn't tell his girlfriend about his plan to marry her, but he could tell her about the nightmares he had about her.

"Mary, since the end of November, I've been having nightmares about you. These nightmares come at me every two weeks. They are always about me betraying you behind your back with another girl, you find out about the affairs, you leave or you end up dead! In some dreams, you dump me for another guy and in another dream you get married, but not to me, but another guy!"

Mary, horrified and in shock that her boyfriend would have terrible dreams about her as she listened to them.

"When I wake up from these dreams, I get sick, so sick that I throw up. That's why you caught me in the bathroom tonight, because I had another nightmare about you." William finished up his story.

"Oh Will, why didn't you tell me these dreams before when this first started?" Mary, with concern.

"I just didn't want you to worry about me otherwise it'll interfere with your work and I didn't want you to be stressed out like I am right now." William hugged Mary.

"You know Will, you can always tell me everything. You don't have to keep secrets from me." Mary stroked William's hair and cheered him up.

"I know. I should always tell you everything, because I trust you. Come on babe, let's go back to sleep. I worried you too much already." Will looked at his girlfriend and took her back to the bedroom.

Thursday was Christmas Eve, William and Mary were at Mary's childhood home for her parent's annual Christmas Party. The Radcliffe's were all happy that Mary reconciled with her boyfriend.

"Come on William, don't be nervous about your proposal. I hope you are not having second thoughts about marrying my sister." Kaylin cleaned the dining room.

"No, I'm not having second thoughts about my proposal. I'm just nervous about it that's all." William looked at the ring.

"Like I said before, you don't have to be nervous. Look, my sister deserves you and you deserve her. You guys belong together and that's the truth." Kaylin walked out of the room.

"You know, Kaylin's right. I have to stop being a coward and propose to Mary in front of her family!" William walked into the kitchen.

After all the presents were unwrapped, everyone talked in the living room and looked at their gifts.

William took a deep breath, and made his move.

"Mary, there is something that I need to tell you. Mary, ever since we got back together in June, I knew in my heart that I couldn't live without you. You were always there for me when I needed help. I know that I made a full-time commitment to you and I want to keep going with this." William got up, knelt down on one knee in front of Mary, and showed her the ring.

Mary looked at Will with shock and at her family, who just looked at her with smiles and shocks.

"Mary, I want to spend the rest of my life with you and I'm proving it with this ring. You are just a beautiful, amazing girl to have in life and I am lucky to have you in my life. Mary, I love you more than anything in the world. Will you marry me?" William poured out his heart to Mary.

Mary sat in her seat, stunned as she looked at her boyfriend. She loved William with all her heart and she wanted to spend the rest of her life with him, but she had to think about his proposal for a couple of minutes.

"Yes William, I will marry you!" Mary smiled.

"Mary, thank you for making me the luckiest man tonight." William took the ring out of the box, placed it onto Mary's left finger, and kissed her hand.

As soon as Mary looked at the ring glowing, her body disappeared leaving a blue orb in her chair. Everyone disappeared and the room turned black. Gabrielle appeared with a smile on her face.

"Will, you did it! You completed your second mission and proposed to Mary. I am so proud of you that you got Mary's dream of being a teacher and a life with you!" Gabrielle congratulated William.

"I am so happy that I completed this mission. I only have three missions to go." William happily picked up the blue orb.

"Are you ready to go on the third mission?"

"Yes, I am Gabrielle. What's the next mission?" William gave the blue orb to Gabrielle.

"The next mission goes one year later where Mary is twenty-six years old."

CHAPTER THIRTEEN

Mary, A Singer

Gabrielle and William teleported to an apartment complex in 2016.

"Gabrielle, who's place is this?" Will looked around the apartment.

"This is your place William. You live here in Cleveland, Ohio."

"What? I don't live in Lake Park anymore." William, with shock.

"Nope. You moved out of Lake Park when you were nineteen and came to Cleveland to start over without anyone that you cared about. Right after high school, you started drinking and hanging around the wrong people."

"I started drinking!" William freaked out.

"Yes, when you started drinking, all your anger stored up inside you and you took it out on your loved ones including Mary. You see when you graduated high school, Mary was your girlfriend. One night during her senior year when you were helping her with her homework, you took your anger out on her." Gabrielle took Will into a flashback.

"Mary, I don't care what happens in my life! I just want to drink and that's all I care about!" William threw Mary's homework all over her room and yelled in front of her.

"Okay Will, calm down please. I was just wondering what you were doing for college. That's all." Mary with fright and picked up her papers.

"Calm down Mary. Are you telling me to calm down? I'll give you calm down!" William angrily walked up to Mary, slapped her, and began to beat her.

"No Will... please stop! Don't touch me! Get off of me! Help me!!" Mary screamed as William continued to hurt her.

Suddenly, Andrew and Petra came barging into their daughter's room to find out what all the commotion was.

"Get off my daughter! Get off of her!" Andrew yelled and pushed William off of the terrified Mary.

"Mary, Mary, are you okay?" Petra hugged her sobbing daughter.

"You get out of this house now before I call the police! I don't want you near my daughter or else I will arrest you! Do you understand!" Andrew threatened William.

"I understand, I understand how a complete loser and stupid your daughter is that I'm through of being her boyfriend for good!" William walked out the door.

After the door slammed shut, the room went black.

"Oh my god, I can't believe I did that to Mary. I abused her!" William with guilt.

"All because of your drinking problems William. By the time you were twenty, all your friends abandoned you and you couldn't see Mary anymore. Your parents kicked you out of the house, because you were causing trouble and getting arrested. So, you decided to go to Cleveland to start over. Once you got to Cleveland, you realized that you were alone and you had a problem. You decided to stop partying, drinking, and go back to school."

"I did? I went to college?"

"Yes, you did. You applied to Ohio State College and went there for four years. You earned a degree in Accounting and started working full-time as a bank teller at the Ohio National Bank in downtown Cleveland."

"But what happened to Mary?" William, with concern.

"Mary? Well, she was mad at you for what you did to her. The next day at Lake Park high, everyone found out about what you did to Mary. Afterwards, Mary got over her anger at you and started missing you when you left town. She met a senior classmate named Alex Hudson in January. After she graduated high school, Mary wanted to become a singer so she decided to form a band with five of her best friends that she can count on the most in the world and became the True Sisterhood Girls."

"Mary became a singer. She made her dreams come true without me and she's friends with one of my best friends."

"She did. The group started in the fall of 2008 with only one song called, Stand By You."

"Who's in the band with Mary?"

"Mary invited Kaylin Robertson, Natalie Bakerson, Jessie Sootburg, Susan Kittle, and Stephanie Berenson to join the True Sisterhood Girl band. By 2012, Mary and Susan worked together to create two new songs called, Always and I am Loving Every Minute Of You. The manager from Capitol Records (Chicago region), Alejandra Mitchell went to one of the band's performances in Chicago in late June of 2013." Gabrielle took William in a flashback when Mary was twenty-two years old.

At the Lake House Club in Chicago, the True Sisterhood Girls were performing, I Am Loving Every Minute Of You when Alejandra Mitchell walked into the club.

"Hey Ron, who's performing tonight?" Alejandra asked the club owner, Ron Perkinson as she listened to the music.

"Oh, that's the True Sisterhood Girls. They are a new pop band that have been playing mostly in all the clubs in Chicago."

"Their music is really good. Are they looking for a record company to promote their music?"

"They are actually. Why don't you talk to Mary Radcliffe after the show? She's the one that formed the band." Ron gave Alejandra her drink.

"Oh I will Ron. It looks like I found my next band to become famous." Alejandra took a sip of her drink.

The show ended around nine, Mary helped her friends put away their music equipment when Alejandra came up to the group.

"Are you Mary Radcliffe?"

"Yes, I am Mary Radcliffe." Mary answered the woman's question.

"I am Alejandra Mitchell, music representative of Capitol Records, Chicago region. I was here at the club during your performance tonight and I think that you and your band have wonderful music." Alejandra introduced herself and complimented Mary and the band.

"Thank you Ms. Mitchell, I am proud of my friends and how far we've come in our music career." Mary happily to Alejandra.

"Are you looking for a record company to promote your band and your music?"

"Yeah we are. The other record company, Jive Records turned us down yesterday and we are looking for another record company." Mary told Alejandra that her band was having a tough time finding a record company.

"Why don't you let me have a copy of your songs and I'll promote them. Maybe we'll have them on the radio. Here's my card. Call me tomorrow and we'll discuss the plans for your band." Alejandra gave Mary her card.

"Okay, thanks Ms. Mitchell. I will."

The flashback stopped on Mary smiling and then it all went black.

"You see the next day, Alejandra met up with Mary and the Sisterhood Girls at her office to sign a contract and signed them to Capitol Records. One year later, the girls had two songs on the radio and they were almost finished with their first album called, Broken Hearts. Now, the Sisterhood band is famous and they are currently on their first tour around the country. They already hit five states and they are going to complete the tour in New York."

"What am I suppost to do in this mission?" William asked as his apartment came into focus.

"You need to win Mary back as your girlfriend in this mission. Her band is in Illinois right now. She'll be coming to Cleveland in two days. I will be back in a couple of days to see how your progress is going." Gabrielle disappeared.

Meanwhile in Chicago, Illinois, Mary was at the lakefront with her band and Alex rehearsing for tomorrow's concert at Millenium Park.

"All right girls, great job rehearsing tonight! I am sure we will rock out tomorrow night. The rest of the night is all yours."

Afterwards, Mary and Alex were on top of his truck when Tyler ran from the other side of the beach with Susan.

"Everyone, I have great news. I just proposed to Susan and we're engaged to be married!"

"Congratulations Tyler and Susan!"

Everyone cheered and congratulated Susan and Tyler as they kissed in honor of their new status.

"I can't believe that Tyler proposed to Susan tonight."

"I know, I can't believe it! I am so happy for Susan and Tyler." Mary smiled and looked at her two engaged friends.

"Their dreams are coming true as well as yours Mary." Alex looked at Mary.

"I know Alex. I can't believe I accomplished my dream of becoming a singer along with my friends helping me. You also helped me too Alex." Mary looked at Alex.

"That's what friends are for Mare. You know, I'm glad that I came with you on the concert tour."

"I'm glad you came too Alex. You've been a big help with the equipment and the repairs. You are a really great friend to me. You've been there for me when the band and I were struggling. You are the only person that understands me."

"I know, I understand you, because I care about you." Alex hugged Mary.

"I care about you too Alex." Mary stroked Alex's hair.

The two let go of each other as they looked into each other's eyes.

"Well, its getting late. I better head back to the hotel for the night. I'll see you tomorrow Alex." Mary smiled and got off the truck.

"Do you want me to take you back?"

"No, its okay Alex. I'll be fine walking back. Don't worry about me. See you." Mary calmed Alex down and walked away.

At the Hilton hotel, Alex caught up with Stephanie in the lobby.

"Stephanie, could I talk to you for a minute?"

"Yeah Alex, what's up?"

"It's about Mary. I can't hide this secret from her anymore!" Alex went crazy.

"Calm down Alex. Now tell me, what's the secret?" Stephanie walked Alex outside.

"Well, the truth is that I'm in love with Mary. I'm crazy in love with her. I loved her since we graduated high school. I tried to tell her how I feel about her, but I always chicken out. I want to ask Mary out, but I can't find a way to tell her. Can you please help me out Stephanie?"

"You're in love with my best friend?"

"Yes, I am in love with Mary. I've been there for her since the band started and I like Mary very much. Please help me win Mary's heart?" Alex begged Stephanie.

"Okay Alex, I'll help you win Mary's heart." Stephanie calmed Alex down.

CHAPTER FOURTEEN

Old Friends Meet Again

Thursday, June fifteenth, 2016 around six' thirty, William walked out of the gym at the Port Community Center and looked at the bulletin board. He noticed a poster of Mary and the True Sisterhood Girls promoting their tour coming to the Summit Theater in Cleveland.

Mary was in Columbus right now and the last city in Ohio she would perform in is Cleveland. She would be in Cleveland for three days before heading to Texas.

William looked at Mary's face on the poster. She smiled, sang her song, and she was still in the picture.

"I know that I hurt Mary before she became a singer. I was stupid, mad, and drunk when I abused her. I need to make it right again between me and her."

William noticed that tickets were being sold at the Summit Theater and today was the last day to buy tickets.

"I have to go see Mary's performance on Saturday night and apologize to her for what I've done to her. I don't know if she'll forgive me or not, but its worth a shot." William looked at the poster.

William headed straight to the theater to get a ticket before they were all sold out.

Later on, William washed the dishes when Gabrielle appeared.

"Well, I see you bought a ticket for Mary's performance on Saturday." Gabrielle looked at the ticket.

"Huh? Oh, hi Gabrielle. You startled me! Yes, I bought a ticket so I can see Mary again." William put the last dish in the dishwasher.

"I'm proud of you Will. You really do love Mary. Oh, here's something that I have for you after the concert on Saturday." Gabrielle gave William an envelope.

He opened the envelope to find a backstage pass to the True Sisterhood concert.

"Gaby, I can't believe that you are giving me a backstage pass for Saturday." Will looked at the pass with amazement.

"I wanted you to see Mary after the concert so you can apologize, catch up, and maybe get back together with Mary. Its what Mary would have wanted."

"Thank you Gabrielle. I appreciate this gift."

"Its no problem at all. I'll be back on Sunday to see how the mission is going." Gabrielle disappeared.

Friday afternoon at the Ohio National Bank, William spotted a familiar face. Stephanie Berenson walked into the bank, went up to the teller line, and Will called her.

"Stephanie Berenson! Long time no see." William looked at his old friend.

"Oh my god, William Valmont! Is that really you?" Stephanie looked at William.

"Yes, it's me." William smiled.

"Oh my god! You look great! How've you been?" Stephanie, with surprise.

"I've been good. I stopped drinking for ten years now. I went to Ohio State College for four years and got my Bank Teller certification. Three years later, I earned Certified Bank Teller's Certificate. Now, I work at this bank for five years and I'm happy with my life. So anyways, how've you been Stephanie?"

"Well after graduation, I joined Mary's band and I stayed with my boyfriend, Joey Summerton. We got married in April of 2015. I'm happy with Joey and the reason why I'm here at the bank is that I'm saving enough money to rent an apartment in Cleveland. You see, Joey wants to settle down in Cleveland and I decided to quit the band at the end of the summer tour. I haven't told Mary about this yet."

"How is Mary?"

"Oh, she's fine. You know, she was mad at you for two months after what you did to her. Afterwards, when I told her that you were kicked out of your house, she was worried about you. You know, Mary misses you, thinks about you everyday, and wonders where you are."

"I guess I really let Mary down. Didn't I?"

"Yes, you did Will. You need to talk to Mary and apologize to her for what you did to her. Hey, are you going to our performance on Saturday? You might have a chance to talk to Mary." Stephanie handed him her check.

"Yeah, I am going to your performance tomorrow night." William gave Stephanie her money.

"Great. See you tomorrow night. I hope you can get to Mary, before Alex gets to her first. See you later William." Stephanie put her money in her purse and walked away.

"Wait a minute! Steph, who's Alex?" William ran after her.

"You don't remember Alex Hudson? He was a good friend of yours before your drinking problem. He's one of Mary's close friends she met during our senior year of high school. Alex told me a few days ago that he has a crush on Mary and that he wants to go out with her. William, I'm sorry to tell you this about Alex, but I think you and Mary belong together. Not Mary and Alex." Stephanie touched Will's shoulder and walked out of the bank.

For the rest of the day, William was depressed. He couldn't concentrate on his work and he kept on messing up. Around one' fifteen that afternoon, he took his lunch break.

"I can't believe one of my friends is trying to get Mary and I thought I was going to win Mary back easily, but I was wrong. I need to win Mary's heart before that Alex takes her away from me! I never meant to abuse Mary. I was so stupid to do that to her. I have to talk to Mary after the concert tomorrow night. I have to apologize to Mary and tell her how much I miss her and how much I love her, because I don't want to lose her again." William ate his lunch.

CHAPTER FIFTEEN

Reunion

Saturday, William thought about of what he'll say to Mary after the concert.

That evening at the Summit Theater, there was a crowded auditorium waiting for the concert to begin. The lights dimmed in the theater, the stage set, and the equipment in place.

"Ladies and gentlemen, welcome to the Summit Theater! Tonight, we are proud to present the True Sisterhood Girls!" The announcer yelled as the girls ran onto the stage.

"Hello Cleveland! Are you ready to rock with us tonight!" Mary yelled into the microphone.

The audience shouted and cheered for the band to play their music while Mary laughed and smiled.

"Then, let's get this party started! Hit it guys!" Mary looked out into the crowd.

Natalie started the drums as the girls played, "Rock The Party".

William, looked at Mary with amazement on how much she changed since the last time he saw her. Mary, glamorous in her black Capri leggings and a dark purple shirt. Her hair was straightened and let down. There were no scars on her body or her face.

An hour later towards the end of the concert, The Sisterhood Girls finished up, "Darkness". Mary, in a pink shirt and a black short skirt looked out into the audience smiling when she spotted William in the first row.

Mary stared at him for a couple of minutes while her band mates looked concerned for their leader.

"Oh my god! William Valmont is here… at my concert! How did he know that I was a singer?" Mary continued to sing and looked away from William.

"All right everyone, this next song I'm going to sing is, The World Is With You." Mary looked at William again.

At the same time, William stared at Mary. He gave her sad looks on his face and she stared back with an apologetic look on her face as she sang the song.

"Oh man, what am I going to say to Mary? I feel so nervous right now that I can't think straight! Looking at her face again is making me happy again, but I feel so guilty and mad at myself for hurting her!" William looked at Mary while she danced and sang on stage.

"All right everyone, this is the end of the night! I would like to sing one more song before you guys go home. This last song I would like to dedicate to is for an old friend of mine out there for me when I needed him the most. Wherever he is, I hope you are all right and I am always thinking about you everyday. This song is for you." Mary dedicated, "Til There Was You" to William.

After the concert, William headed backstage to find Mary. He found Stephanie putting the equipment away.

"Hey, I see you made the concert. Did you see Mary yet?" Stephanie looked up to find William next to her.

"I did see Mary during the concert, but I haven't talked to her yet."

"I couldn't believe she dedicated, "Til There Was You" to you. This means that she still has feelings for you. You better tell her your feelings before she moves on with her life." Stephanie warned William.

"I will. I'm going to talk to her right now, but I just don't know what to say to her. I mean, I have my apology, but I don't know what to say afterwards."

"Just be yourself William. Tell Mary how deeply you feel about her and how much you want her." Stephanie told William to focus.

"Thanks Steph. Where's Mary's dressing room?" William with confidence.

"It's down that hallway. First door to the right."

"Thanks. I'll see you later." William smiled and walked away.

"Good luck Will. I hope you'll be Mary's boyfriend by the end of the night." Stephanie smiled.

"I hope so too Stephanie." William walked down the hallway.

Not too long afterwards, Stephanie placed her keyboard in the case when Alex came up to her.

"Hey Steph, you guys were awesome tonight!" Alex looked at Stephanie.

"Hey Alex. What's with the flowers?"

"Oh, these roses are for Mary. She deserves them since she did an awesome performance tonight. Did you tell Mary my feelings for her yet?"

"Not yet Alex. I mean, we've been so busy with the performance that I couldn't tell Mary anything."

"It's okay Steph. I'm just going to tell Mary everything now anyways. Thanks for helping me though. Catch you later." Alex walked away.

"Wait Alex! Mary has company!" Stephanie tried to stop Alex.

Alex didn't hear Stephanie's words and gone down the dressing room hallway.

"I hope William gets to Mary before Alex does." Stephanie panicked and looked down the hallway.

In the fourth dressing room down the hall, Mary dressed in a purple t-shirt and black satin pants retouching her make up when she heard a knock at the door. Mary opened the door to find William there.

"Hi Mary." William stared at Mary with a saddened look.

"Hi William." Mary, with a calm stunned look.

They looked at each other for a couple of minutes until Mary rushed into William's arms. Mary exploded herself into William as they embraced.

William was happy to have Mary in his arms again. The memories of him being an abuser and abusing Mary were erased by Mary's hug.

"Oh William, how did you know that I was a singer?" Mary continued to hug William.

"One of my old friends told me what you were up to over the last ten years. That's why I'm here tonight at your concert, because I wanted to apologize to you for what happened during your senior year in high school. I wasn't thinking straight and I was selfish. When I came to Cleveland after my parents kicked me out and I was still an alcoholic, I realized that I was alone and I had no one. So, I decided to quit drinking, went back to school, and decided to become a bank teller. I also got a job and turned my life around. The only thing that I didn't have was you. I know that I hurt you in the past and it was a big mistake. I am so sorry for ever laying a hand on you and abusing you. Will you ever forgive me?" William begged forgiveness.

"I forgive you William. I can't believe you changed and I'm so glad that you..." Mary touched Will's face and stared into his eyes with a smile.

Before Mary could finish, William kissed Mary on her lips.

The two kissed for a couple of minutes until they broke apart. Mary felt light-headed and in her mind, she remembered when she and William dated.

"Mary, are you okay? It looks like you are trembling." William, with concern.

"Huh? Yeah, I'm okay. Do you want to come into my dressing room so we can talk?"

"Sure." Will followed Mary into her dressing room.

"So Mary, what happened during your senior year that I missed out on?" William sat down on a couch next to Mary.

"The day after you abused me, I went to school miserable and bruised. I was mad and blamed myself for letting you abuse me. I was mad at you for letting you drink and turning your life in a bad direction. Afterwards, I moved on. I met new friends and accomplished my dream of becoming a singer. You know, over the last ten years, every day I kept on thinking of you and I wondered where you went. Sometimes, I even wondered if you were hurt or killed somewhere, because of your alcohol problem. I thought I lost you for good. I thought I was never going to see you again."

"Mary, I am so sorry for getting mad at you and abusing you. I shouldn't have never done that. I was so stupid for turning to alcohol and taking my anger out on you and my friends. I didn't want to hurt you at all, because I loved you too much. I didn't want to change at all. I wish I could go back in time and redo everything and still be with you. I didn't want to hurt you, I wanted to love you. "

"Oh William, I…" Mary blushed pink in her face.

Before Mary could tell her feelings to William, there was a knock at the door.

"Who is it?"

"It's me Mary, Alex. I need to give you something." Alex, from outside the door.

"Okay, I'll be right out. Will, I'll be right back." Mary got up from the couch.

"Here Mary, these are for you. You put on an excellent performance tonight." Alex went red in the face and he gave Mary a bouquet of pink roses to her.

"Thanks Alex. These flowers are beautiful." Mary smelt the flowers.

"Mary, the reason why I pulled you out of your dressing room is that I wanted to tell you something." Alex quietly.

Meanwhile, William waited for Mary to come back, overheard Mary and Alex's conversation outside. He walked over to the door and listened.

"Mary, I know we've been friends for eight years now and I've been there for you when you started your music career and when your band was struggling. You see, after the first year you became famous, I started to have a crush on you. Mary, remember the concert in Chicago?"

"Oh my god, Alex likes my Mary!" William panicked.

"Yes, I remember the concert. Why do you ask?"

"The day before the concert after the rehearsal we were talking on the head of my truck, I wanted to tell you how much I liked you, but I couldn't do it, because I was scared to tell you. Now, I can finally plucked up courage tonight and I want to ask you something. Mary, will you go out with me?"

"Oh my god! Two guys like me! I can't believe this. I still have feelings for William and I have feelings for Alex, but I only like Alex as a friend. I can't choose who I want right now. I need to think about this…" Mary stood there.

"Alex, I don't know what to say to you right now. Let me think about this first and I'll tell you my answer when I made my decision."

"It's okay Mare. There's no rush. Just tell me your answer when you made your decision." Alex calmed Mary down, kissed her cheek, and walked away.

William, still listened had peeked through the keyhole and saw Alex kissed Mary.

"I can't believe Mary chose him over me! I guess it was a waste of time coming to her performance tonight and told her my feelings. She only wants Alex and that's fine with me!" William walked away from the door, heartbroken.

Mary opened the door to find William still on the couch.

"William, I'm sorry that took too long." Mary walked to him.

"Yeah, so you can accept Alex's proposal to go out with him instead of me!" William ignored Mary.

"William, are you okay?" Mary, with concern.

"I thought you had feelings for me Mary! I thought you wanted me to come to your performance… and I was going to give you another chance, but I see it was all for nothing!" William sadly looked at Mary.

"Will, what are you saying? Where is this coming from?" Mary, with a puzzled look on her face.

"You know exactly what I'm talking about Mary! I heard your little conversation with Alex and I heard everything!"

"Oh Will, don't say that. I didn't say yes to Alex. I told him that I need sometime to think about it." Mary explained herself.

"I don't want to hear it Mary! You love Alex now! You don't love me anymore! I'm sorry for wasting my time and I'm sorry for coming back into your life." William bitterly stormed out of the dressing room.

"William, wait please! I can explain!" Mary ran after William, but he was already gone when she got into the hall.

CHAPTER SIXTEEN

I Am Going To Make A Decision And I Choose...

At the Asterview hotel an hour later, Mary was in her room moping, feeling miserable, and mad at herself for making William upset.

Meanwhile, Kaylin worried about her friend ever since they got back from the Summit Theater.

"Mary, Mary, are you okay? Can I come in?" Kaylin knocked on the door.

"You can come in Kay." Mary laid down on her bed.

"Hey, how are you doing? What's wrong?" Kaylin closed the door and sat next to Mary on the bed.

"Kaylin, do you remember William Valmont?"

"Yeah, I remember that jerk. Why do you ask?"

"He was at our performance tonight."

"What!" Kaylin freaked out.

"Yes, William was there. After the concert, he came to see me. He told me that he stopped drinking and turned his life around. He went to college and got his certification as a bank teller and he's currently works at the Ohio National Bank. Will also told me that he didn't want to hurt me and that he still has feelings for me."

"Oh my god! How did he find out that you were a singer?"

"I don't know Kaylin, I don't know. Before I could tell William my feelings for him, Alex knocked at the door. I told Will to wait while I talked to Alex. Alex told me that he wanted to go out with me and he has a crush on me. Now, I feel torn between Alex and William. I told Alex that I needed sometime to think. Somehow, William listened in on the conversation and got upset that Alex wanted to ask me out and he stormed out. I didn't even get a chance to tell him how much I still love him." Mary moped into her pillow.

"I'm sorry that things didn't turn out the way you wanted, but you still have Alex, Mary." Kaylin placed her arm around Mary and hugged her.

"I don't love Alex Kaylin! I love William! Look, I just need to be by myself right now to think about my decision." Mary sobbed as she let go of Kaylin.

"Okay, but I hope you okay for tomorrow's concert."

"Don't worry, I'll be okay." Mary wiped her tears with a Kleenex.

Kaylin closed the door and walked back to the living room to find Stephanie watching TV with her husband.

"Hey Kaylin, is Mary okay?" Stephanie, with concern.

"No. Apparently, William Valmont appeared at our concert performance tonight to see Mary. He tried to ask Mary back out, but I guess he overheard Alex telling Mary that he wanted to go out with her. William got upset and stormed out on her."

"You mean William tried to ask Mary out?"

"Yes, he tried to but… Hey, how do you know about William trying to ask Mary out? Did Mary tell you?" Kaylin, with confusion.

"Actually Kaylin, I caught up with Will yesterday. You see, I bumped into him at the Ohio National Bank. I told him that Mary misses him and she wondered where he has gone to in the last ten years. I also told Will about Alex having a crush on Mary."

"Steph, are you going to tell Mary what happened on Friday, because you need to tell her." Kaylin, anxiously.

"I will tell Mary right now." Stephanie got up and walked over to Mary's room.

"Mary, it's Steph. Can I come in?" Stephanie knocked on the door.

"Yes, you can come in."

"Hey, Kaylin told me what happened tonight. I can't believe that Will did that to you." Stephanie walked over to Mary's bed and hugged her.

"I know and I wanted to tell him how much I still love him."

"Look Mary, yesterday, I was at the bank and I ran into William. He told me what he's been up to and he still loves you."

"Oh god! I wish that Alex didn't tell me his feelings for me! I have to tell William that I love him and only him, but I wish I knew where he lives at so I can tell him."

"I know where he lives Mare. He told me after the concert before he saw you. He lives in an apartment complex called, Highland Creek. The complex is on Dewford Road. It's not too far from the hotel. Maybe tomorrow we can go talk to him and straighten this mess out." Stephanie cheered Mary up.

"Okay. I'll go with you. So I can try and talk to him." Mary wiped her eyes.

Monday around ten' thirty, Stephanie took Mary to the Highland Creek apartment complex to catch William before he went to work.

"Here, apartment 27C on the third floor." Stephanie looked at the directory.

"Okay. Come on, let's go up there." Mary walked up the stairwell.

Meanwhile, William put on his tie when he heard the doorbell rang. He opened the door to find Mary and Stephanie at his door.

"Stephanie, Mary, what are you guys doing here?"

"Will, Mary needs to talk to you about what happened last night after the concert. Can we come in?"

"Yeah come in."

"Okay Mary, tell him what you said to me last night." Stephanie put her hand on Mary's shoulder.

Mary looked at Stephanie for a few minutes, who gave her a smile to pluck up courage. When Mary looked at William, he had anger in his eyes as he placed a calm facial look on his face. Mary felt guilty after she looked at William as she took a deep breath and spilled out her words.

"Will, I know that you are mad at me for what happened after the concert last night, but I am going to make a decision whether I should be going out with you or Alex. I just need sometime to think and I'll…" Mary explained to William.

"Look Mary, I have had enough of your lies and games! I can't take it anymore!" William snapped at Mary.

"I'm not lying to you Will. I'm just saying that I need time to choose the guy I want to be with!" Mary defended herself.

"I don't want to hear it Mary! Look, just go be with Alex. Be his and forget that I ever came back into your life! I gotta go to work." William, coldly and walked out the door.

"I don't want Alex. I just want you!" Mary shouted and ran into the hallway after William, who was already in the elevator.

Mary looked at the elevator feeling terrible and depressed that she wouldn't be able to win William back.

"I guess I came here for nothing." Mary, sadly as Stephanie came out into the hallway and closed the apartment door.

"I am so sorry Mary, for dragging you out here for nothing." Stephanie hugged Mary and tried to cheer her up.

"I think I made my decision, Steph."

"Okay. Come on, let's get out of here." Stephanie placed her arm around her friend and they walked to the elevator.

That evening, while Will washed the dinner dishes, white smoke filled the kitchen and Gabrielle appeared with an angry look on her face.

"William! How dare you hurt Mary and let her go like that?"

"I had to let Mary go, because she likes Alex Hudson! Not me!" William shouted and sat in the kitchen chair.

"Oh William. Mary doesn't like Alex. She likes you."

"Yeah right Gabrielle. I can't even tell if Mary is telling the truth to me or not!"

"You know, I was there when Mary was with Alex the night after the concert. When Alex asked Mary out, I was inside her mind and the person she was only thought of was you. You see William, the only person that Mary loves is you! You didn't want to hear her real feelings for you, because you were worried about Mary going out with Alex and not you."

William looked at Gabrielle for a few minutes and everything fell into place.

"Oh man, I really screwed up this time with Mary." William woke up from his altered state.

"Yes, but you can still win Mary back, but you better do it quickly before she leaves tomorrow for Texas." Gabrielle warned William.

"Oh my god! I have to go see Mary at the hotel before she leaves tomorrow and I'll lose her forever!" William panicked.

"Wait a minute! Will, do you even know where Mary is staying at?"

"Oh crap! No I don't. I completely forgot to ask Stephanie where she and Mary were staying at on Saturday!"

"William, don't give up yet, because I know where Mary is staying at."

"Where is she staying at?"

"She is staying at the Asterview Hotel which isn't far from the Summit Theater."

"Thank you Gabrielle. I promise I will fix my relationship with Mary and we can be together again."

Meanwhile, Mary and her band mates were at the hotel packing up their suitcases after their final performance in Cleveland.

"Hey Mary, how are you doing? Stephanie told me what William did to you today. Are you okay?" Jessie walked into Mary's room.

"I'm all right Jess. After the performance we did at the Indian Point Theater, I forgot all about what William did to me and got me thinking of the rest of the tour coming up in Texas." Mary packed up her clothes and hair stuff.

"Will doesn't deserve you Mary and besides, if you two got back together, he would've started drinking again and hurting you like before back when we were seniors in high school." Jessie felt happy for her friend.

"I know Jessie and tomorrow, I'm going to tell Alex my decision at the airport." Mary packed her make up bag in the suitcase.

"What are you going to tell him Mare?"

"You'll see tomorrow Jess." Mary smiled.

Tuesday, William drove over to the Asterview Hotel to catch Mary before she headed to the airport.

"Excuse me, can you tell me which room is Mary Radcliffe and her Sisterhood band are staying in?"

"Let me check. I'm sorry, but Ms. Radcliffe and her band have already checked out of this hotel. They were heading to the Navaport International Airport not too long ago."

"Okay. Thank you very much." William rushed out of the hotel.

Meanwhile, Mary and her friends waited at gate 18 for the boarding call to be announced. Mary sat in the chair area with Jessie and Kaylin. Alex was over by the window looking out into the airfield.

"Well, here's your chance Mary. Tell Alex your decision." Kaylin looked at Alex then at Mary.

"I don't know you guys. What if I'm making the right decision. Now go over there and tell Alex." Jessie assured Mary.

"Okay, here it goes." Mary got up from her seat.

Meanwhile, William rushed through Navaport Airport. He looked at all the flight schedules and found out that American Airlines flight number 327 to Houston was leaving in five minutes.

"I have to get to Mary before I lose her again forever!" William panicked and ran through the airport trying to find gate 18 in the American Airlines section.

"Alex, there is something that I need to tell you."

"What is it?"

"I finally made my decision and the person that I choose to be with is…"

"Wait Mary! Wait!" A voice called out to Mary.

Mary and Alex turned around and noticed William running into the gate area.

"William, what are you doing here?"

"I'm here, because I don't want to lose you again, Mary."

"I don't want to hear it William! You hurt me for the last time and I don't want to speak to you anymore!" Mary turned away from William and looked at Alex.

"Please Mary, I am so sorry for hurting you and not believing your feelings for me. I was just too worked up that Alex asked you out and I thought you were going out with him but I was wrong. If you don't want to speak to me again, I understand." William walked away.

"Wait William! Why would you think I would go out with Alex?" Mary turned away from Alex and looked at William.

"I thought you had feelings for Alex and I also thought you wanted to be with him. Mary, I still have feelings for you even though I hurt you in the past. That night when I saw you during your performance, I fell in love with you even more than the first time I laid eyes on you. I want you back Mary and I promise that I'll never hurt you again."

Mary looked at William with a smile on her face while Alex looked at them with anger.

"Okay Mary, it's time to choose! Who's it going to be?" Alex walked up to Mary with fury.

"Okay Alex. The person that I want to be with is... William."

"What! Why would you choose him over me when he abused you before and he might to it again to you!"

"Look Alex, I know that you are a nice guy, but I have no feelings for you. The only person that I have feelings for is William Valmont. I know that William abused me in the past, but he apologized to me after the concert Saturday night at the Summit Theater. He told me his feelings for me and I told him that I still loved him and thought about him every night after he abused me. I always loved William and I'll love him for the rest of my life. I'm sorry Alex, but I only like you as a friend." Mary looked at Alex and then at William.

"Fine Mary! If that's what you want then I'm sorry for ever walking into your life! I'm out of here forever!" Alex stormed out of the gate area.

Mary ran into William's arms, happy that they were back together again.

"Attention please, flight number 327 from Cleveland to Houston is now boarding."

"Mary, it's time to go. The plane is boarding." Natalie walked up to her friend.

"Listen Natalie, tell everyone to go on without me. I want to stay here in Cleveland with my boyfriend." Mary looked deeply into William's eyes.

"Mary, what about the concert at the Alamo next week? We can't go on with the show without you." Natalie persuaded Mary to go to Texas.

"Don't worry Natalie, I'll be in Texas a day before the concert. Just lead practices like you always do when I'm not there. I'll rehearse while I'm in Cleveland and I'll come down to Texas in a couple of days." Mary reassured Natalie.

"Okay Mary, I'm so happy that you and William are back together. See you in a couple of days." Natalie hugged her friend goodbye.

"Mary, I can't believe that you are going to stay in Cleveland with me." William happily held Mary in his arms.

"I wanted to stay so we can spend sometime together. Afterwards, I'm taking you down to Texas and you can see the rest of the tour." Mary touched William's face.

The two grew closer to each other until William kissed Mary, the kiss of true love promising Mary that he will always love her and never hurt her again.

Suddenly, Mary's body disappeared and a red orb was on the floor. Will picked up the red orb and the airport went into a blackened state.

"Well William, you did it! You completed your third mission. You have Mary's dream of becoming a singer, being Mary's boyfriend, and being by her side." Gabrielle appeared in the darkened area.

"Thanks. You know, I thought I was going to fail this mission." Will held the glowing orb in his hands.

"Are you ready to go on your fourth mission?" Gabrielle took the red orb and put it into her dress pocket.

"Yes, I'm ready."

"Let's go three years into the future where Mary is twenty-nine years old." Gabrielle took Will's hand and took him into the future.

CHAPTER SEVENTEEN

William's Sudden Change

G abrielle and William arrived in a mental hospital room where there
was a bed, bedside table, a barred window, and another little room
which was a bathroom.

"Gabrielle, where are we?" William looked around the dark, lonely
room.

"William, this is the Valley Lake Mental Hospital outside of Lake
Park."

"What? Why am I in this dreaded place?" William walked towards
the window.

"The reason why you are here William is that you turned your life
the wrong way after you graduated high school."

"What did I do?" William, with concern.

"Well, let's go back a few months after graduation. You were driving
home from Lake Park Community College, one of your tires ran over
a nail and blew out. Luckily, a guy named Devon Peterson come to
your rescue and gave you his spare tire. At his house, this is where your
sudden change comes into play."

"Thanks for helping me Devon. I'll let myself out." William grabbed his
book bag.

"Will, wait a minute! I want you to try something." Devon cornered Will by the door and gave him a lit- rolled up piece of paper.

"What is this?" William looked at the rolled up piece of paper.

"Just take a puff and tell me what you think."

After the first puff, William felt like he wasn't there anymore. He felt loose and brainless.

"This is awesome. You have to give me more of this stuff! It's so good!" William looked at the paper, and fell in love with it.

"Sure. Here's a week's worth of weed. Come back if you need anymore." Devon gave William a brown paper bag.

The flashback stopped and Gabrielle and William came into view.

"I turned to drugs! You've got to be kidding!" William looked at himself with the bag of weed in his hand.

"Yes William. You tried Marijuana and cocaine. Soon after, you started mixing alcohol with the drugs. By the time October came, Mary discovered your problem." Gabrielle showed William another flashback.

"William, what is this?" Mary picked up an empty vodka bottle from underneath his bed.

"It's nothing Mary, honestly." William lied to Mary.

"What's that underneath your breath? Is that alcohol? Have you been drinking?" Mary, with suspicion as she smelt Will's breath.

William just stood there as he looked at Mary with guilt.

"Tell me the truth Will! Are you drinking alcohol?"

"Mary, I can't lie to you, but I have been drinking and using drugs for four months. One of my friends got into drugs and drinking and I liked doing it since the first day." William confessed.

"Why would you do this to yourself? You were doing so good after high school! I can't believe you turned to drugs!" Mary held up a bag of cocaine.

"Mary, I'm sorry. Please, I'm trying to stop drinking and doing drugs. Will you forgive me and help me quit my addictions?" William begged Mary.

"No William no! You will not drag me into your world of drugs and alcohol and that's a world that I don't want to be in! I need to break up with

you William. Goodbye!" Mary threw the bag of cocaine at William and walked out of his room.

The room faded into darkness and William and Gabrielle came into the room.

"I can't believe I lost Mary to my addictions. I am so stupid!" William, angrily pounded the darkened walls.

"Yes and the break up took a huge toll on you that you continued to do drugs and drink. You started on crystal methane, you moved out of your parent's house and moved in with Devon, joined in Devon's gang called, The Brothers of Destruction, you abandoned all your friends, dropped out of college, and abandoned your future."

"What happened to Mary after she broke up with me?" William, concerned about Mary.

"Well after the break up, Mary moved on without you. In December, she met someone else at the Snow dance at Lake Park high."

"Oh come on Mare. Try and have a good time tonight." Sarah encouraged her friend.

"Yeah, let's go dance!" Jessie grabbed Mary's arm and dragged her to the dance floor.

Mary danced with Sarah, Jessie, Natalie, and Susan. They tried to cheer her up after the break up with William two months ago. Mary was in a short, dark purple dress with silver high-heeled shoes and her hair up in a bun.

After dancing to three songs, Mary walked off the dance floor over to the snack area to get some punch.

Over by the punch bowl, a guy named Daniel Potter filled up his cup when he noticed Mary.

"Here, take this. I saw you out on the dance floor, you must be tired." Daniel gave the cup to Mary.

"Thanks. Yeah my friends dragged me to the dance floor. They are trying to cheer me up after my break up with my boyfriend a couple of months ago."

"Same here. My date dumped me for someone else she met a couple of days ago."

"Damn! That sucks. Hey, why don't we sit down at that table and we can talk some more."

"Okay." *Daniel walked over to a table near the dance floor with Mary.*

"So, what's your name?"

"Oh, my name is Daniel Potter. What's your name?"

"I'm Mary Radcliffe."

"That's a nice name Mary. So, tell me what happened between you and your boyfriend?"

"Well his name was William Valmont and after he graduated from this school, he started using and doing drugs and drink alcohol. When I discovered the drugs and alcohol, I was devastated. I had to break up with William before he dragged me into a world of drugs and alcohol."

"Oh man, I'm so sorry Mary. I wonder why he would turn to drugs and alcohol in the first place?" *Daniel disgusted with the story.*

"I don't know. I don't even want to think of what he's doing now or where he is now." *Mary sadly thought of William.*

"Mary, hey, hey, its okay. You made the right decision to break up with your boyfriend so that you couldn't be in a place where you could get hurt. It's not your fault that he took his life down the wrong path in the first place." *Daniel tried to comfort Mary.*

"Yeah, you're right. Thanks Daniel." *Mary hugged Daniel.*

"No problem Mary. Hey, will you dance with me?"

"Yeah, sure." *Mary smiled.*

Daniel took Mary's hand, led her to the dance floor, and slow danced with her.

Natalie, at a table with the others, noticed her friend dancing with a guy.

"Hey Sarah, Susan, Jessie, look who's dancing out on the dance floor!" *Natalie looked out onto the dance floor.*

"Oh my god, Mary is dancing with a boy!" *Susan, happily with shock.*

"I knew that taking Mary to this dance would cheer her right up." *Sarah looked happily at her friend dancing.*

The scene stopped where Daniel and Mary danced and gazed into each other's eyes.

"The next day at lunch, Daniel surprised Mary with a pink rose and asked her to be his girlfriend." Gabrielle narrated the next flashback with Daniel and Mary.

"Oh man, Mary moved on in her life and who knows what the hell happened to me!" William, ashamed of himself.

"Well, you continued your ways and Mary graduated high school with her boyfriend. She attended Lake Park Community College and took her general classes. She got a job as a day care worker for Children's Heart's Day Care Center during the days before she went to college."

"She got her life while I slacked around being an idiot!"

"Will, let's go back three years and see what your future has for you." Gabrielle teleported Will into the future.

They arrived at a Halloween Party in an empty bedroom at Devon's house. William, dressed up in a pirate costume with black pants, black boots, a white silk dress shirt, and a fake sword.

"William, this is where I leave you. I'll see you back at the mental hospital when you get there."

"Okay, I'll see you there." William acted gangly.

After Gabrielle left, William walked out of the bedroom and went downstairs to the party.

"Hey Will, I want you to meet a new member of our group." Devon placed his arm around his friend.

"Dev, I don't think I'm ready for this." William disbelieved his friend.

"Look, I know that Kristy dumped you, but its time to move on with life! Will, I want you to meet Kayla Hampshire."

A girl who was nineteen was talking to her friends when Devon and William approached them. She was dressed as a vampire princess in a black short dress with black flat shoes.

"Kayla, this is our best gang member, William Valmont."

"Hey, it's nice to finally meet you Will. I've heard a lot about you even though its been a week since I joined this gang." Kayla smiled at William.

"Thanks. I heard a lot about you too." William looked at Kayla.

"Well, I'll catch you later then. Come on Jen, let's go dance." Kayla walked towards the dance floor.

"Oh come on Will! Ask Kayla for a dance. I know you have a crush on her. You've been crushing on her ever since you first laid eyes on her. While you are dancing, tell her how much you like her."

"Okay, I'll ask her, but first give me a beer." William stared at Kayla as she danced on the dance floor.

Devon handed William a plastic cup of beer. Will drank half of it and walked to the dance floor.

"Kayla, would you like to dance with me?" William blushed.

"Sure I'd love to." Kayla blushed.

The two started to dance fast at first, but for the rest of the time, they slow danced.

"You know Will, the gang told me a lot about how you always win fights, turf battles, and never got caught by the police. How do you do it?"

"Well, I used to always get myself in trouble when I was younger and I always got away with everything."

"Wow. You know, I've always liked that with guys. The type that are bad and who always get away with things." Kayla looked into William's eyes.

"Well go on wuss! Tell her how much you like her!"

"You know Kayla, ever since you joined the group, I developed a crush on you. Every time I tried to tell you my feelings, I chicken out."

"Will, there's something that I need to tell you too." Kayla blushed.

"What is it?'

"I developed a crush on you ever since the first day I saw you. I wanted to tell you my feelings, but you were going out with someone else and I thought I would never have a chance with you."

William looked at Kayla for a minute, placed his finger underneath her neck, raised her head, and kissed her.

The two kissed for the longest time, passionately and romantically while Devon and the rest of the gang cheered for William's victory.

"Let's go upstairs to my room." William smiled at Kayla while he stroked her hair.

"Okay." Kayla smiled as Will led her hand and hand upstairs.

After William closed his door, he looked at Kayla, and kissed her.

"Woah, wait a minute Will. Do you think you are going too fast?" Kayla sat on the bed.

"Oh no of course not! We like each other right?" William panicked.

"I do like you Will. I like you so much that I want to go out with you." Kayla touched William's face.

"Really. You want to go out with me?"

"Of course I do Will. I want to be your girlfriend, because I love you." Kayla poured her heart out to William.

"I love you too Kayla. Come here." William walked over to Kayla and kissed her.

"Oh Will, I…" Kayla began.

"Shh Kayla. Let me prove my love for you is real." William looked into Kayla's eyes as he unzipped her dress.

Kayla kissed Will as she unbuttoned his shirt and fell onto the bed.

William took off Kayla's dress and kissed every part of her body.

"Will, are you really sure you want to do this with me?" Kayla stopped William as he kissed her neck.

"Yes, I am sure that I want to prove myself to you. I promise that I won't hurt you and I'll do anything for you. If you want me to stop, I'll stop." William pulled away from Kayla.

"No Will don't stop! I'm sorry for being insecure like this. You can continue. I won't stop you." Kayla longed for William.

William continued to kiss Kayla as he unfastened her bra. Before long, they both consumed themselves and their love for each other.

CHAPTER EIGHTEEN

Good Times Gone Bad

Two weeks after meeting at the Halloween party, William and Kayla were a couple. Kayla moved out of her friend's apartment and moved in with her boyfriend and his best friend.

One Saturday night while William and Kayla slept, Kayla woke up nauseous.

Kayla ran over to the bathroom, sat on the floor, and threw up. After five minutes, Kayla flushed the toilet, thinking why she was throwing up all of a sudden.

"Okay, it couldn't have been the food I ate tonight and I'm not sick then... oh no! I hope I'm not... pregnant! Please I hope not, because I don't want to have kids." Kayla panicked as she continued to sit on the floor.

Sunday morning, Kayla ate breakfast when Devon entered the kitchen.

"Hey Kayla, later on, don't forget to go to Langston Park to beat out our rival gang okay." Devon went into the refrigerator.

"I will. Um, Devon, could you do me a huge favor?" Kayla put her spoon in her cereal.

"What's the big favor?" Devon grabbed a beer.

"Devon, I need you to go get me a pregnancy test." Kayla spilled out her secret.

"What! You mean, Will knocked you up!" Devon, after he drank a sip of beer from the bottle.

"I think he might have knocked me up. Just please, let's keep this a secret until I know that I am really pregnant with my boyfriend's child."

"Okay, I'll keep this our secret." Devon reassured Kayla as he placed his arm around her.

Later on, Devon went to CVS to get the pregnancy test for Kayla. Before William got home from working at Wickerson's Market, she took the test.

After three minutes of waiting, the results came in. Kayla looked at the test, then at the box, and dropped everything to the ground.

"Oh my god! I cannot be pregnant! I can't believe it!" Kayla panicked and sat on the bathroom floor.

"I know my boyfriend wants to have a family and I don't want to have any kids in my life. Maybe I should get an abortion… no I can't. I have to keep this baby for William's sake." Kayla touched her stomach.

A few minutes later, Kayla came downstairs to the living room where Devon was.

"Well, what were the results?"

"I'm pregnant Devon. I am officially carrying William's child."

"Wow. Are you going to tell him about the bun in the oven?" Devon sat on the couch.

"Yes I will as soon as Will gets home from work."

"Are you going to keep the baby or terminate it?"

"I don't know Devon, but I will get an abortion if Will doesn't want to be a father. If he wants to be a father, then I will go through the pregnancy."

"Well you better think of a way to tell him, because he just pulled into the driveway." Devon looked out the window.

"Oh my god! I can't go through with this!" Kayla panicked and got up.

"Kayla, you can't run away from this! You have to tell Will the truth." Devon tried calmed Kayla down.

"Hey, what's up everyone." William walked into the house.

"Hey um, you know what, I'll leave you two alone so you guys can talk." Devon looked at William, Kayla, and left the room.

"Will, there is something that I need to tell you."

"What is it?"

"Ever since that night we hooked up and became a couple, something happened to me. Since the last two days, I've been getting up late at night and throwing up. Today, I told Devon to go get me a pregnancy test at the drugstore. Before you came home from work, I took the pregnancy test and found out that I am carrying your child Will."

"This is great! Now we can have our family together like I always wanted." William hugged his girl.

"Yeah, our new family." Kayla with guilt and shame.

On Tuesday, November 7th, 2011, it was William's birthday. Kayla came home from a doctor's appointment, felt upset. Ever since Kayla told William she was pregnant, she changed dramatically. She used drugs while she carried her boyfriend's child.

"Devon, I don't think I can carry this baby to full-term. I mean, I want to make Will happy, but I don't want any kids." Kayla confided to Devon.

"I know how you feel Kayla. I don't want any kids either. I don't know why Will wants to have a family. I don't know why he joined this gang in the first place or broke up with his ex-girlfriend." Devon sat next to Kayla.

"Kristy Spearson?"

"No, Mary Radcliffe. Before all this happened, Mary turned Will from a troublemaker into a good person. You know, sometimes he still thinks about her and wonders what she's been up to. Will is so complicated to have as a friend."

"I know Devon. You know, I'm starting to regret that I hooked up with Will. I should've hooked up with you."

Suddenly without thinking, Devon kissed Kayla. They kissed for a couple of minutes passionately until they broke apart.

"Oh man, I'm sorry for kissing you like that."

"No, it's okay Dev. I'm not mad at you." Kayla touched Devon's face.

"No, I'm sorry. I have to go." Devon got up from the couch and walked out the front door.

Kayla got up from the couch and went upstairs miserable. She went into her room to take a nap. She slept through the afternoon, swimming into dreams of what could've happened to her. She woke up at eight that evening to find the house still empty. William was at a party that his friends threw for him for his birthday.

"I am so sorry baby and I'm so sorry Will. I can't deal with being pregnant and raising a family. I give up." Kayla touched her stomach and she looked at a picture of her boyfriend in tears.

Kayla got up from the bed, walked over to William's desk, opened the desk-side door, and pulled out a handgun.

"Goodbye Will, I'm sorry that I'm not the right girl for you." Kayla cried, pointed the gun at her stomach, and shot herself.

Kayla fell to the floor and blood went all over the place.

An hour later, William came home.

"Kayla, Devon, are you guys here?" William took off his jacket and went upstairs.

William opened the bedroom door to find Kayla on the floor in a pool of blood.

"Oh my god, no, no, no, Kayla! Please don't be dead! Oh god!" William cried, yelled, and held Kayla in his arms.

William got up from the bloody floor, picked up the gun from Kayla's dead hand, walked over to a mirror in front of the dresser, and threw the gun at the mirror. Glass shattered all over the dresser and onto the floor. William picked up a piece of glass and slashed both his arms.

"Hello? I'm home. Anybody here?" Devon walked into the house.

William sat on the floor dripping blood everywhere. He grabbed the gun and pointed it at his head. Before Will could pull the trigger, Devon walked into the bedroom.

"What the hell? Will, put the gun down!" Devon ran up to his friend.

"No! I don't want to! I want to kill myself just like how Kayla killed herself!" William yelled and held the gun in his hand.

Devon tried to get the gun out of William's hand, but he kept on backing away from Devon.

The two struggled as they fought to see who was going to get the gun until a shot was fired. William fell to the ground with a bullet lodged in his left arm.

Devon ran downstairs to the living room where the phone was at and dialed Markus's number.

"Markus, you need to get the boys and come over to my place right away."

"Yeah, what's going on?"

"Just get over here right away. We need to get some vermin out of my house."

Twenty minutes later, Devon waited by the window until he heard knocking at the door.

"Hey, what's going on?" Markus walked into the house.

"Its Kayla and Will! We have to get them to the hospital right away!" Devon ran upstairs while the gang followed.

They ran upstairs into William's bedroom and discovered the gruesome scene.

"Oh my god! Okay, we'll load them up and get them to the hospital!" Ashton panicked and looked at his friend.

The brothers helped load Kayla and William into Markus's truck and drove off to Sheridan Memorial Hospital.

Meanwhile, Mary got out of her Child growth and development class at Lake Park Community College.

"Hey Mare, how was class for you today?"

"It was pretty interesting after the surprise pop quiz we had at the beginning of the class, but it was a great day. How was math and drama class?"

"Math was boring today. My professor gave the class chapter fifteen for homework, but drama class pretty interesting."

"That's good Natalie. So, what are your plans for tonight?" Mary walked out the front entrance with Natalie.

"Oh well, I'm going to go out with Scott tonight. He's going to pick me up right now. You want him to give you a ride home?"

"Actually, Daniel is taking me out tonight. He's taking me on a moonlit walk through Langston Park and then he's taking me to the new pizza place that just opened."

"Aww, that's so romantic. Infact, here comes your boyfriend Mare." Natalie looked at the entrance.

"Hey sweetheart! Hey Natalie! How was class?" Daniel walked up to Mary and Natalie with a bouquet of pink roses.

"Hey babe. Thank you for the flowers they are gorgeous. Class was pretty good today. Natalie's classes were all right until her drama class."

"Drama class was pretty exciting, at least we didn't have homework tonight. All I want to do is hang out with my girl. Let me go get my car Mare. I'll be right back." Daniel kissed Mary's lips and walked away.

"Okay." Mary smiled.

"So… It looks like things between you and Daniel are blossoming." Natalie looked at her friend.

"Yes. We've been going out for almost three years and I couldn't be more happier with Daniel." Mary sighed and watched Daniel walk over to his car.

"Say Mary, don't get mad, but do you still think about William sometimes and maybe wonder what he has been up to?" Natalie walked down the entrance steps.

"You know Natalie, I do think about William, but I don't want to know what he has been doing since our break up." Mary looked up into the sky.

Meanwhile at Sheridan Memorial Hospital in trauma room one, Doctor Stevens operated on Kayla.

"What do we have here?"

"We have a nineteen year old woman with a gun shot wound to the stomach. Doctor, she's also pregnant." The nurse put on her gloves.

"All right, let's try and save her and the baby!" Dr. Stevens placed an oxygen tube down Kayla's throat.

Before Dr. Stevens could cut Kayla open, she went into a cardiac arrest.

"I need the defibrillator right now!" Dr. Stevens dropped the knife.

The nurse handed the doctor the defibrillator and tried to revive Kayla.

"Doctor, forget it. She's lost a lot of blood and her pupils are dilated. She's dead." The nurse encouraged Dr. Stevens to stop.

"Time of death, 7:50PM." Dr. Stevens turned off the heart monitor.

Meanwhile, Dr. Henderson worked on William and brought him to a stable condition.

"All right, let's take Mr. Valmont up to recovery." Dr. Henderson took off his gloves.

The next day, Devon and Markus were in William's hospital room across from his bed.

"Markus, I can't be his friend anymore if he keeps on trying to kill himself." Devon looked at Markus.

"Look Dev, I know that you are heartbroken and torn up about Kayla's death, but you know that this is all Will's fault for doing this to Kayla in the first place."

"I know, I know. Damn it! I wish I could've hooked up with Kayla before Will did. I shouldn't have introduced him to Kayla. I should've just asked her out at the party!" Devon banged the walls.

"Dev, it's not your fault man. Look, I think its time that we abandon one of out members. Even if he is the best in our group. Most of his belongings are in that drawer and the closet. When we get home, we'll get rid of the rest." Markus tired to calm Devon down.

"You know what, you're right. We have to ditch him for what he has done. Mary can take care of Will from now on. Come on, let's do this for Kayla." Devon, angrily as he and Markus snuck out of the room.

Two weeks past, Devon and the Brothers of Destruction never came back to the hospital to visit William.

One Saturday evening, William tossed, turned, and moaned in his sleep. He sank into nightmares about his past. His break up with Mary...

"Mary, please don't do this to me. I don't want to lose you. Don't go!" William begged Mary to stay.

"No William no! I won't let you drag me into your world of drugs and alcohol! I am breaking up with you William. Don't come crawling to me for help if you running from the law!" Mary put her foot down.

"It's not going to be like that Mare, I promise you it won't be. I want to quit all this so I can be good for you again." William took Mary's hands.

"Stop lying to me! You won't change! I can't believe I wasted all this time with you when I could be accomplishing my dreams and I'm not going to let you take all that away from me! Goodbye William forever!" Mary walked out the door and slammed it.

His hook up with Kayla...

"Go on Will! Go ask Kayla for a dance. I know you like her. Tell her how much you like her while you dance with her." Devon encouraged Will.

"Kayla ever since you joined the gang, I developed a crush on you." William told Kayla his feelings.

He looked at Kayla, placed his finger underneath her neck, raised her head, and kissed her.

"Let's go to my room." William stroked Kayla's hair.

"Wait a minute Will. Do you think you are going too fast?"

"Of course not! We like each other right?" William panicked.

"I do like you Will. I like you so much that I want to go out with you and I love you." Kayla poured her heart out to William.

"I love you too Kayla. Come here, let me prove my love for you is real." William looked into Kayla's eyes and he unzipped her dress.

"Are you really sure that you want to do this with me?" Kayla stopped William.

"Yes, I am sure that I want to prove myself to you. I promise that I won't hurt you and I'll do anything for you."

He kissed Kayla as he took off her clothes and consumed himself inside Kayla. Which turned into her suicide...

"I'm so sorry Will. I can't have this baby or go through with our relationship."
Kayla pointed the gun at her head and pulled the trigger.

William woke up with fear in his eyes, but made no sound.
"Why is this happening to me? This is the fourth nightmare I had this
week!" William drank his cup of water and looked out the window.

An hour later, William tossed, turned, and dreamed about Mary.
"I still think about William, but I don't want to know what he has been
up to." Mary's voice rang out in William's mind.
He pictured himself walking down a long hallway. The halls were painted
black and the lights dimmed.
"Where am I? How long is this hallway anyways?" William continued to
walked down the hallway.
He came up to a black closed door. He opened the door to find Mary alone
at a table dressed in a short purple dress with her hair let down half straightened
and half curled as William walked up to her.
"Mary? Mary! Thank goodness I found you! You have no idea what I've
been through the last few days." William happily hugged Mary.
Mary didn't hug Will back. She looked right through William as though
he didn't exist.
"Mary, its me William Valmont, you're old boyfriend. Can you see me?
Can you hear me?" William looked at Mary and panicked.
Mary got up from the table and walked to the center of the room, a light
shined down on her.
A hand came out of the darkness and Mary took the hand. Daniel came out
of the shadows and began to dance.
William watched in silence as Mary danced with Daniel as they kissed on
the dance floor. Will picked up a gun right next to him, looked at Mary for the
final time, and shot himself in the head.
William woke up again with fear and tears ran down his face.
For the rest of the night, William sat in his bed keeping himself
awake so he wouldn't have another nightmare.

By lunch the next day, William tried to go to sleep, he'd pinch or
slap himself to stay awake.

"Why should I go through this? Having these nightmares and keep myself awake? I know my friends ditched me and I lost everything. Why should I be alive and got through all this pain and suffering?"

Will took a butter knife from the lunch tray and before he could slit both of his wrists, the day nurse came into his room.

"William, what are you doing?" The nurse walked up to the bed.

"I don't belong here anymore. I don't deserve to live! I have no one in my life." William, in a trance-like tone.

"No, don't say that. You do deserve to live. Just put down the knife and everything will be okay." The nurse tried to stop William from committing suicide.

"No! I just want to die!" William raised the knife.

The nurse went outside the room, raised a code red, and the medical team rushed into the room.

"No please! I just want to die!" William yelled and screamed as the doctors strapped and held him down on the bed.

Doctor Henderson put the knife on the tray and gave William a sleeping shot.

"What are you going to do with Mr. Valmont, doctor?" The nurse held Will's hands.

"Well, since we've been observing Mr. Valmont for the last couple of days, I'm going to send him to the Valley Lake Mental Institution." Doctor Henderson gave William the shot and calmed him down.

CHAPTER NINETEEN

Mary, A Perfect Housewife

Two years past, Mary graduated from Lake Park Community College along with her friends and Daniel.

In their junior year of college, Daniel moved out of his parent's house and into a condo out by Langston Park. Mary moved in with her boyfriend a few weeks afterwards.

"Dan, I can't believe that we graduated college!" Mary took off her silver graduation cap.

"I know honey. I can't believe it either. Hey, anything good in the mail?" Daniel hugged his girl and sat on the couch.

"Well let's see, there's the cell phone bill, college bill, junk, and oh, it's a letter from Columbia Pictures studios in California." Mary looked through the mail.

"What? Here, let me see it." Daniel, with confusion as Mary handed him the letter.

Daniel read the letter several times and turned from confusion to shock.

"Oh my god, I can't believe it!"

"What is it?" Mary, with concern.

"Mary, do you remember that audition for the teen thriller, The Mystery at the Midnight Nightclub?"

"Yeah, you auditioned for that movie a couple of months ago. Why?" Mary looked at Daniel.

"Well, I got the main role as Roger Handcock, the teen detective!" Daniel showed Mary the letter.

"Oh my god, I can't believe you got the part! I am so proud of you!" Mary hugged and kissed her boyfriend.

"I know and this is the start of my acting career! Oh, but the letter says that I have to go to Los Angeles for a year to film the movie." Daniel looked at Mary with a sad look.

"It's okay. You go to Los Angeles. I'll wait for you until you come back. We'll call each other everyday so that we don't lose contact." Mary touched Daniel's face.

"You promise that you won't go out with any other guy while I'm away?"

"I promise I'll stay faithful to you while you are away." Mary touched Daniel's heart.

The months past, Mary kept herself busy at the day care center, paid the bills, and hung out with her friends. She kept in touch with her boyfriend everyday.

It was in April when Mary received a phone call from Daniel.

"Babe, guess what!" Daniel, happily over the phone.

"What is it Dan?"

"I'm coming home the day before my birthday! April fifteenth!"

"Oh my god! I can't believe you are coming home! Wait a minute, the fifteenth is in a couple of days isn't it?"

"Actually, it won't be until next week, but the film is finished and I'm coming home just in time for my birthday!"

"That's great! Oh, I can't wait to see you again! I missed you so much!" Mary grew excited again.

"I know, I can't wait to see you again too Mary. I missed you too much and I can't wait to have you in my arms again when I get home. Hey, I have to let you go, I'm being called on set for the last scene. I'll talk to you later."

"Okay, I love you."

"I love you too Mary. Bye." Daniel hung up.

"So Mary, what's the big news?"

"Daniel's coming home next week!"

"That's wonderful! When's he coming back?"

"The day before his birthday. You know Kay, I want to throw Dan a surprise birthday/welcome home party." Mary thought of an idea.

"That sounds good Mare. You can have the party here at your place and I'll help you plan the party." Kaylin agreed with Mary's idea.

"Great! Let's get started." Mary got out a pen and paper.

On Monday, April fifteenth, 2013, Daniel came home.

Mary met Daniel at O' Hare airport to pick him up.

"Surprise!" Mary said as Daniel came out from the terminal.

"Mary, I missed you so much." Daniel rushed into his girlfriend's arms.

"I missed you too Dan. I'm glad you are back home again." Mary looked into Daniel's eyes.

"Come on, let's go home. I can't wait to tell you about the film." Daniel placed his arm around Mary.

"Hey babe, tomorrow after you get out of the center from your work out, can you come straight home instead of going to Ron's house?" Mary walked over to baggage claim.

"Sure I can. What's going on tomorrow?"

"You'll see" Mary smiled.

Tuesday, April 16th, 2013, Daniel went to the community center, Mary called Kaylin and they decorated the apartment for the party.

"Daniel is going to love this party, Mary." Kaylin placed the food on the table.

"I know, this was a great idea for me to throw a party for my boyfriend." Mary set up the drinks.

Around 4:45, everyone was there waiting for Daniel to arrive.

"Okay everyone, Daniel's home! Tyler, you get the lights. When Daniel opens the door, Tyler will turn on the lights, and we'll all yell surprise." Mary told the plan to everyone.

As Daniel opened the door, Tyler turned on the lights.

"SURPRISE!" Everyone yelled and came out of their hiding places.

"Wow, this is a surprise!" Daniel dropped his gym bag on the floor.

"Hey, it was your girlfriend's idea to throw this party for you Dan." Ron smiled at Mary.

"Oh thank you Mary so much for this party!" Daniel hugged his girl and gave Ron his gym bag.

"Hey, It's no problem. I wanted to make your birthday a special day for you." Mary kissed her boyfriend.

During the party, Mary went into the kitchen to get the birthday cake while Daniel and Ron were in Daniel and Mary's room.

"Ron, I've been thinking ever since the last three days I came back from LA in February, I got a present for Mary. Remember that one Saturday we went to the mall?" Daniel looked through his desk drawer.

"Yeah, when we went to Kay Jewelers. I remember. What kind of present did you get Mary?"

"Since Mary and I have been together for five years now, I bought her this engagement ring." Daniel pulled out a dark royal blue ring box, opened it, and showed Ron the seven carat diamond ring.

"Oh wow! Daniel, are you going to propose to Mary?"

"Yes, I am Ron. Tonight, right after the party. I'll propose to her." Daniel looked at the ring.

The party continued until nine. After everyone left, Mary cleaned up the apartment while Daniel washed the dishes.

"Okay, I am going to propose to Mary tonight no matter what happens. I have to do it." Daniel walked out of the kitchen.

"Mary, thank you so much for this party tonight. You really made my birthday special." Daniel surprised Mary as he held her.

"It's no problem baby. I wanted to make your day a very good one this year for you." Mary looked into Daniel's eyes.

"Mary, I need to tell you something." Daniel smiled.

"What is it?" Mary touched Dan's face.

"I know we've been going out for almost six years now and these years with you have been great. You mean everything to me and I think about you all the time. When I was in LA, I thought about you all the time and I never wanted to be without you. Every time I'm with you, you brighten up my life, you give me ambition, and you give me happiness. I am ready to make a full-time commitment to you. Mary, you are the perfect girl for me and I want to spend the rest of my life with you. Mary, will you marry me?"

"Oh Daniel... yes, I will marry you!" Mary accepted Daniel's proposal.

"Mary, you are just an amazing girl that I ever met and I am so glad you came into my life." Daniel placed the ring on Mary's left ring finger and looked into her eyes.

"I know and I am glad that we are getting married!" Mary wrapped her arms around Daniel's neck.

After months of planning, Daniel and Mary had their wedding on Thursday, July seventeenth, 2014. The ceremony took place at the pavilion bridge in Langston Park.

"Do you Daniel Robert Potter take Mary Petra Radcliffe to be your wife?" Pastor Peter performed the ceremony.

"I do." Daniel looked at his bride.

"Do you Mary Petra Radcliffe take Daniel Robert Potter to be your husband?"

"I do." Mary smiled at her boyfriend.

"I now pronounce this lovely couple as husband and wife! You may now kiss the bride." Pastor Peter concluded the ceremony.

Daniel and Mary kissed each other as their families and friends clapped and cheered for their new life together.

"I pronounce you Mr. and Mrs. Potter!" Pastor Peter announced as Daniel and Mary broke apart and walked down the aisle.

At the reception in the pavilion, everyone celebrated Mary and Daniel's new status.

"Oh Mar, I am so happy for you!" Susan hugged Mary.

"Oh thank you Sue! I am so happy that I married Daniel!" Mary looked at her husband.

"Attention everyone, as Daniel's best man, I would like to propose a toast to my best friend and his wife! Daniel and Mary, I wish you the best in your marriage! I want you to have many happy years together and have wonderful memories together! To Daniel and Mary!" Ron held up his glass and toasted to his friend.

"Now, as Mary's maid of honor, I would like the bride and groom to have their first dance as husband and wife." Natalie stood next to Ron on the balcony.

Mary and Daniel walked over to the dance floor as the DJ put on a slow, romantic song and the lights went dim.

"Honey, how are you doing? Are you enjoying our new life together?" Daniel danced with his wife.

"I am Dan. This has been the happiest day of my life. I am so glad that you chose me to be your wife and I am so happy to be with you." Mary kissed her husband as Daniel held her close to him.

Meanwhile, William was in his hospital room at the Valley Lake Mental Hospital. He's been at the hospital for four years now. He was diagnosed as an alcoholic and a drug addict.

During the time William was in rehab, he met a girl named Shannon Taylor. She was a drug addict when she came into Valley Lake.

"So, what are you in for?" William asked Shannon after they got out of their rehab session.

"Oh my parents placed me in this facility after they found my stash of cocaine in my make up case and they thought I was going crazy. How about you? What are you in for?"

"Drug addiction, alcohol problems, and suicidal watch. I was in a gang before I came here. I was doing drugs, alcohol, and causing a lot of trouble. On my 24th birthday, my girlfriend decided to kill herself along with my unborn child she carried out of the blue. When I found her, I wanted to kill myself, but I was stopped. While I was in the hospital, my friends ditched me, and I had nightmares every night that I wanted to kill myself, because I had no one."

"Oh, I'm sorry William about your baby. Just when you were going to change your life around. You know, if I was your girlfriend, I wouldn't have killed myself. Hey, I gotta go to another group session. I'll see you later." Shannon walked away.

"Okay, I'll see you around." William blushed and watched Shannon walk away.

By the time 2013 came, William improved, he went out with Shannon, and was happy. Shannon looked exactly like Mary in Will's eyes, but deep down, he still loved Mary.

Meanwhile, Shannon grew tired being in the mental hospital that she wanted the easy way out.

In late June, Shannon waited for William to get out of his therapy session.

"Babe, I have great news! My therapist told me that I have only one session with him and he might release me in two weeks!"

"That's wonderful hon. I'm so proud of you!" Shannon hugged her boyfriend.

"I know and you should be getting out soon right?" William touched Shannon's face.

"Well, Dr. Terry says that I need more therapy, because I've been taking a turn so I might need to stay here a little bit longer." Shannon explained to William the situation.

"I'm sorry, but don't worry. I will find a place for us and I will find a job to support you."

"Babe, could you do me a huge favor?"

"What is it?" William, with concern.

"Could you go to the Nurse's station and get me a pair of scissors. I want to trim my hair, because I don't like this length at all!" Shannon looked at her hair.

"Oh okay. I'll do it."

"Thanks babe. I'll see you with the scissors at lunch." Shannon kissed William on the cheek and walked away.

That evening, Shannon looked at a bracelet William made for her a couple of months ago.

"I'm sorry William, but I can't be with you. I'll be stuck at this dump for the rest of my life. I rather be dead then to be in this place!" Shannon placed the bracelet on her bedside table and picked up the scissors.

"This is for the best of me... I guess. Goodbye cruel world and my love." Shannon sat on her bed and slit her wrists.

The next morning, Nurse Jane, came into Shannon's room to find a pool of blood. She found Shannon in her bed, blood dripped from her wrists.

Jane pushed the red button on the wall and the medical team rushed into the room.

"Forget it everyone. Ms. Taylor is dead. Call the coroner Janie." Doctor Terry took off her gloves.

William walked down the hall to Shannon's room to get her for breakfast. He noticed that Shannon's door was closed. He opened the door to find Shannon's body on her bed.

"Shannon? Oh no... not this again! No! Oh god!" William ran to Shannon's bed side and broke down.

Doctor Terry walked into the room with the coroner and found William there with Shannon.

"Mr. Valmont, I'm so sorry, but Ms. Taylor is dead. We concluded that she killed herself before she fell asleep last night. I know that Shannon meant a lot to you William, but she started to decline after she feared that she'll never get out of Valley Lake."

Days went by, William regressed after Shannon's funeral. Dr. Arborson diagnosed him as an insomniatic and possibly suicidal. After Shannon's death, William had nightmares again about Mary and Shannon. William didn't sleep for almost a year now and withdrew into himself.

On July seventeenth, 2015, Daniel and Mary celebrated their first wedding anniversary together.

"Hon, that was a delicious dinner. This has been the most special day that we had together since we got married." Mary started the dinner dishes.

"Mary, there is something that I need to tell you that will make this day even more special." Daniel helped his wife with the dishes.

"What is it?" Mary turned off the water.

"Mary, since my acting career is taking off and there's income coming in, I was thinking that we should move to San Francisco, California so that I can be near Los Angeles and be near you when I'm filming a movie." Daniel suggested to Mary.

"Really? California? I would love to move to California with you. I know Sarah and Jeremy are out in San Francisco so I can see them again. Yes, I want to go Daniel." Mary happily agreed to her husband.

"That's it then, we are going to California!" Daniel hugged and swung Mary in his arms.

Two years later, Daniel and Mary settled down in a cozy neighborhood in San Francisco. Mary caught up with two of her old friends, Sarah Hagerton and Jeremy Jensen. They lived next door when Mary and Daniel moved to town.

"Mary, I am so happy that you married Daniel! I wish that Jeremy and I could've come to your wedding, but we had class that whole week."

"It's okay Sarah. I'm not mad at you for not coming to the wedding. I know that you and Jeremy are working towards your florist and business careers and I understand that. Thank you for the lovely picture frame." Mary opened Sarah and Jeremy's gift.

"Your welcome Mare. You know, it's been a long time since I've been going out with Jeremy and I'm ready to have a full-term relationship with him." Sarah thought about her boyfriend.

"Are you serious Sarah? Are you sure that you want to be with Jeremy for the rest of your life?" Mary, with concern.

"Yes. We are both ready to be in a full-time relationship. I just wish that Jeremy would propose to me soon." Sarah wondered.

"Don't worry Sarah, he will. You'll see." Mary patted Sarah's shoulder.

That same time, Mary was seven months pregnant with Daniel's child while Daniel tried out for a few parts in LA.

"So Dan, did you receive any word on the production companies that you auditioned for movie parts yet?"

"Not yet Mare. I'm starting to think that I'm not going to get any parts in any movies." Daniel helped his wife into bed.

"Don't say that Daniel! Don't ever discourage yourself! You will get the part babe. Never give up! Especially with our baby coming soon." Mary reassured Daniel.

"You're right babe. I want to keep my acting career going and I want our new family to be proud of me. I'll just keep waiting until I get a part." Daniel touched Mary's stomach and looked into her eyes.

Two days later, Mary prepared lunch in the kitchen when the phone rang.

"Hello."

"Hi, is Mr. Potter there? This is Mr. Brian Cashman from Warner Brothers Pictures and I want to talk to him about his audition from last Thursday."

"Yes he is. Let me go get him." Mary told Mr. Cashman to hold for a minute.

"Daniel, Mr. Brian Cashman is on the phone. He wants to talk to you about your audition from last week. Maybe you got the part." Mary said as Daniel walked into the kitchen.

"Hello, yes Mr. Cashman. Yeah, I auditioned for the part of Adrian Bowes last week. Yes, are you serious? Really, yeah, I will be there in June. Okay, thank you. Bye." Daniel happily hung up the phone.

"Well, what did he say?"

"Mary, I got the part in Running Out of Time and filming starts next month!"

"Oh my god, that's wonderful! See, I told you, you were going to get the part! I am so proud of you!" Mary hugged Daniel.

"I'm so happy too! Now my career is rising again just in time for our baby to be born." Daniel touched Mary's stomach.

In June, Daniel filmed down in LA. Mary read on the sofa with Sarah when she felt something wet.

"Sarah, I think my water broke! I think its time!" Mary panicked.

"Okay, okay, I'll get you to the hospital." Sarah grabbed her friend's suitcase and helped her to the car.

"Honey, I'm having the baby!"

"Really! Okay, I'm on my way! Don't have the baby until I am by your side." Daniel panicked over the phone.

"Okay, I'll try. I'll see you soon." Mary hung up her phone.

At St. Sinah Hospital, Mary was in the Maternity Ward in Labor.

"When is Daniel coming? I need him!" Mary screamed as Dr. Stacey Nolan told Mary to push.

"Don't worry Mare, Daniel will be here in a couple of minutes." Sarah got off Mary's cell phone and went by her side.

"Okay Mary, this is it. I need you to take a big push on this contraction." Dr. Nolan looked at the monitor.

"Okay."

Before Mary could push, Daniel walked into the hospital room.

"Hey baby, I'm right here. Did I miss anything?" Daniel kissed his wife.

"You didn't miss anything Daniel. Mary is just about to deliver your baby. I'll step out into the hall and I'll let you be alone." Sarah walked out into the hallway.

"Daniel, I thought you weren't going to make it here in time." Mary happily held her husband's hand.

"Me too dear, but I didn't want to miss the birth of our first baby." Daniel rubbed Mary's forehead as she pushed.

"Okay Mary, you are doing a great job. Now, all we need is one final push and the baby will be out."

Mary pushed her final push as Daniel stayed by her side as they heard crying in the air.

"Congratulations, you have a baby boy!" Dr. Nolan cleaned up the baby and gave him to Mary.

"Oh Dan, look at our child. He looks just like you." Mary smiled and looked at her baby.

"He does. What are we going to name our boy?" Daniel looked at his son.

"Deacon, Deacon Daniel Potter." Mary announced their new baby's name.

After Running Out of Time was completed, Daniel moved onto his third role as Brandon Ericson, a teacher who helped his classmates overcome hard times during a nation's crisis. It was in 2017 when Jeremy and Sarah got married. Mary quit her job at Kindercare, became a homemaker, and took care of Deacon.

"You know Mary, we are the two most luckiest women in the world." Sarah sat on the front porch while Deacon slept in his mother's lap.

"We are Sarah. We have wonderful husbands, building our families, and having perfect lives." Mary rubbed her son's head.

"Yes and I can't wait for my little bundle of joy to be born!" Sarah touched her stomach.

"Having kids is fun Sarah, but we have a responsibility to take care of our children. I don't want Deacon and my future children to go down a road where there are bad things. I want them to have good futures just like how Daniel and I have right now." Mary picked up Deacon and held him.

"You know Mary, you are a terrific mother. You always look out for your kids and give them potential for their future. Mary, I want you and Daniel to be godparents to my child when it comes." Sarah announced to Mary.

"Oh my gosh, thanks Sarah. I promise that I will be a great godmother to your kids. I won't let you down." Mary hugged Sarah.

"I know you won't let me down, because you are my friend." Sarah looked at Mary with a smile.

On Tuesday, October 11th, 2018, Mary was in the bathroom. For the last two days, Mary felt sick and very tired. She decided to take a pregnancy test, because she started to have the funny feeling before she found out she was pregnant.

After two minutes of waiting, Mary looked at the test and noticed the strip turned blue.

"Oh my god! I knew it, I knew that I was pregnant. I had almost the exact signs when I first carried Deacon. Daniel is going to be so happy that we are having our second child!" Mary smiled and looked at the strip.

Daniel came home after he ran to the market to get some groceries.

"Hey honey, how are you doing? How's our Deacon doing?" Daniel kissed Mary's cheek.

"Deacon's good. He's in the yard on the swing. Babe, I have great news." Mary glowed at Daniel.

"What is it hon?"

"Remember when I got sick and I found out that I was pregnant with Deacon. Well… I'm pregnant!" Mary showed Daniel the test strip.

"Oh my god, I can't believe it! Our second child! Honey, I'm happy for us!" Daniel hugged Mary happily.

"I know… I can't believe that are family is almost complete!"

On Wednesday, June fifth, 2019 at St. Sinah hospital, Mary went into early labor.

"Congratulations Mary, you have a healthy baby girl!" Dr. Nolan gave Mary her newborn baby.

"Oh Mary, our daughter looks just like you . Beautiful and stunning just like the first time I laid eyes on you." Daniel admired his daughter and he kissed Mary's forehead.

"Daniel, she has your bright blue eyes. You are just the sweetest man!" Mary held her daughter in her arms.

"I wonder what are we going to name our daughter?" Daniel asked as Mary gave him their girl.

"I decided that we should name her Natalie Susan Potter. I gave her that name in honor of my two friends, Natalie Bakerton Jacobson and Susan Kittle Hagerton. The ones who brought us together in high school." Mary smiled and looked at her baby.

CHAPTER TWENTY

A Surprise Visitor

Back in Illinois at Valley Lake Mental Hospital, it was Tuesday, December 25th, 2018, it was around two in the morning when William came out of another nightmare. This time it was about Shannon's death except, William killed Shannon instead of Shannon killing herself.

"Stop letting me have all these nightmares! I am going insane! I just want my life back... the one I never shared with Mary!" William begged and prayed on the floor.

"You need to get better William! I need you to get better." A voice called out to William.

"Who's there? Who are you? Show yourself!" William called out to the mysterious person.

"William, it's me, Mary... you do remember me... do you?" Mary answered William's questions.

William looked at the window to find Mary on the bench looking at him.

"Mary, I can't believe that you are here right now and you still look the same the last time I saw you." William walked over to Mary and hugged her.

"I know... I'm still the same Mary that's been waiting for you all these years while you were in this place." Mary held onto William and stroked his hair.

"I know you have and I'm sorry for making you wait all these years. I did a lot of stupid things and left you hanging, but I want to get better so I can get out of this place." William touched Mary's face and smiled at her.

"William, I need you to get better so that you can see me again. So we can have our life that we wanted together." Mary looked at William with a sad look on her face.

"I don't think I can Mare. I keep on having nightmares about you and they keep coming at me constantly and I just can't stop having these nightmares." William spilled out everything to Mary.

"I'll be your guardian angel William. I'll watch over you and every day and I'll take away all your nightmares, so you can be free." Mary looked into William's eyes as her nose touched his nose.

"Really? You will watch over me and protect me?"

"Yes silly, because I love you William and I don't want to lose you." Mary smiled at Will and kissed him.

William kissed Mary harder and held her face. He stroked her hair as Mary stroked Will's hair.

"I'm going to make you healthy again William. I won't let you have another nightmare again, I promise. If you ever need me… I will be in your heart to guide you." Mary touched William's heart.

William looked at his heart and when he looked at Mary, she was gone.

The next morning, William woke up refreshed and all the stress melted away from him.

Since then, William stopped having nightmares and thoughts of suicide. He attended all his rehab, therapy, and group sessions. He stopped thinking of his past with the Brothers of Destruction, Kayla, his unborn child, and Shannon. Mary protected William as she promised him.

In July 2019, Dr. Arborson saw William's dramatic change.

"William, I am proud of you. You've healed and rehabilitated into a new person. I think you are ready to leave Valley Lake mental center." Dr. Arborson told William after the therapy session.

"Really, I can finally get out of here?"

"Yes, you can. You've inproved in all of your sessions. I don't know why we should keep you here any longer. I'll sign the release forms tonight and you'll be released tomorrow." Dr. Arborson got out the forms.

"Thank you Dr. Arborson. I promise you that I won't go back into my old habits and end up back in here again."

"Well, I hope I don't see you here again William. I don't want to make a bad decision to release you." Dr. Arborson looked at William

"Don't worry Doctor, I won't mess up again. I promise. I'm devoting myself to have a better life without drugs and alcohol. I just want to focus on the life I never got to have with the one girl who has been there for me ever since I first met her."

"I hope you do get to see that person. That was a very touching story William. It's settled then. Tonight is your last night here at Valley Lake." Dr. Arborson signed the release forms.

Later that evening, William looked out his window at the stars.

"I can't believe I'm getting out of here tomorrow! The first thing I have to do is see Mary and apologize to her for the mistakes I caused to break us apart." William walked to his bed, and fell asleep.

Thursday, William took a bus back to Lake Park to the east side. He got off on Shore Lane and walked towards Mary's house.

"Okay... once I get to her house, I'm going to apologize to Mary for being selfish and not being there for her all these years. Then maybe we can try and repair our relationship." William walked up the driveway.

"William... stop! Don't ring that doorbell!" Gabrielle appeared.

"Why Gabrielle? How come I can't see Mary?"

"Mary doesn't live here anymore."

"What?"

"Mary doesn't live here anymore. You see, while you were in the mental hospital... things changed. Mary graduated Lake Park Community College, married Daniel Potter, and moved to San Francisco, California."

"No, she couldn't have gotten married! No! Please don't tell me that this is true!" William panicked.

"It's true Will. Mary moved on in her life without you." Gabrielle, with guilt.

"I can't believe this! I need to find Mary, Gaby… Right now! I have to go to California and find you!" William begged Gabrielle.

"Okay William. Here's the ticket. The flight leaves in three hours. You better get over to O' Hare airport before you miss the flight. I'll see you when you get to San Francisco." Gabrielle gave William the ticket.

Later on during the flight, Will thought about Gabrielle's words.

"Remember, you can only win Mary back as a friend in this mission. This is just like the first mission. Don't worry and don't let your emotions get in the way. The key is to gain back the trust and the friendship you had with Mary."

That made William panic even more as he looked out the window.

Friday afternoon, Mary was at home having lunch with Sarah and Thomas. Natalie slept in her crib upstairs, Daniel was in LA wrapping up on a tv show, and Deacon played in the backyard.

"So Mary, are you ever going back to work in Day care?" Sarah asked Mary as Mary brought out a jug of iced tea.

"You know Sarah, I don't think I'll be going back to work anymore. I am happy being a housewife and I love to take care of my kids. Besides, Daniel is bringing in good money and we are surviving." Mary poured iced tea into Sarah's glass.

"Sounds like a good plan Mare. You know, after I had Thomas and I went back to work as a florist, it felt weird being away from Thomas. Now, I am used to doing two things instead of being at home all the time." Sarah told Mary as she drank her tea.

As Mary sat down in her chair, the doorbell rang.

"Stay here Sarah. I'll get the door." Mary got up and walked over to the front door.

Mary opened the door to find William Valmont at the door.

"Hi Mary, long time no see." William looked happily at Mary.

Mary stared at William as though this was all a dream. Her heart started to beat really fast and she started to lose her breath. Mary fell to the floor into unconsciousness.

Sarah heard a crash from the other room that she decided to investigate.

"Oh my god Mary! Mary wake up!" William got down on the floor and tried to wake Mary up.

"Get away from her William! Get away from her! What the hell are you even doing here?" Sarah ran up to Mary.

"I wanted to come and see Mary so I can apologize to her for what I've done to her a long time ago." William explained himself to Sarah.

"Yeah right! I don't think Mary wants to hear your lame, lying apologizes. Now, get out this house and don't ever come back into Mary's life again!" Sarah shouted and kicked William out of the house.

An hour later, Mary woke up on the living room couch with Sarah by her side.

"Hey, how are you feeling?" Sarah took the cold cloth off Mary's forehead.

"What happened to me?" Mary looked around.

"You fainted at the front door in front of William Valmont."

"What? Oh my god, so its true... William is here in California!" Mary placed her head in her hands.

"It's true Mare, he is here. I don't know how William found you, but he did. I told him to get out and never come back into your life again."

"Oh... okay." Mary looked at Sarah sadly.

"Mary, are you okay? Do you need anything?" Sarah got up and headed towards the kitchen.

"No actually. I'll be in there in a minute." Mary looked at the floor with disappointment.

"Okay. Take your time."

"I can't believe that William found me after all these years! Why did he show up at my door today? I wonder what he wanted to tell me. I feel so stupid fainting in front of William! I feel so terrible that I let Sarah push and yell William away from me!" Mary, with guilt and continued to look at the door.

That same evening, William was at the Baymont Inn, miserable.

"What was I thinking? I can't believe Mary fainted in front of me when she saw me. I was close to apologizing to her for being a jerk in the past, but I blew it!" William looked up at the ceiling from his bed.

Swirls of white smoke began to fill the room as Gabrielle appeared.

"I see that you made it to San Francisco safely. Did you see Mary yet?" Gabrielle looked at Will.

"I did visit Mary, but the visit didn't go so well." William sat up on the bed.

"What happened?" Gabrielle sat next to him.

"Well, after I checked into the hotel, I went over to Mary's house. When she opened the door, it all went downhill. She took one look at me and she fainted. Soon after, her friend Sarah kicked me out of the house and out of Mary's life."

"Oh my gosh, I'm sorry that had to happen. Are you going to try and see Mary again soon?"

"I don't know yet. I may need a few days until my mind can settle down. Since I just got out of the hospital, I need some rest."

"Okay, I'll let you have a few days to yourself. Whenever you are ready to see Mary, I'll be watching." Gabrielle disappeared.

Monday afternoon, William felt rested and ready to talk to Mary again.

Mary was at home baking sugar cookies while Deacon played in the living room with his friend, David Patterson. Mary washed the dishes when the doorbell rang. Mary opened the door to find William at her doorstep again.

"Hello Mary." William smiled at her.

Mary quickly turned around and tried to close the door when Will grabbed Mary's hand.

"Mary... please, let me explain why I'm here. I just wanted to apologize to you for what I did to you so many years ago. I was stupid for letting drugs and alcohol get the best of me and making us break up. I've changed now and I am free from my addictions. I want to save our friendship and gain your trust again." William begged Mary.

"Okay Will. Come on in. It's good to see you again." Mary let William in, closed the door, and hugged him.

"It's good to see you too Mary. You have no idea the things I faced in my life without you." William let go of Mary.

"I know. Let's go into the kitchen and we'll catch up." Mary led Will into the kitchen.

"So tell me Will, what happened to you after our break up?" Mary poured William a cup of coffee.

"Well the day we broke up, I found myself living with Devon and joining his gang called the Brothers of Destruction. I continued to use drugs, alcohol, and I even mixed drugs with the alcohol. By 2011, I was the best gang member that Devon ever had. I fell in love with a newbie in the gang named Kayla Hampshire. We hooked up at a Halloween party at the end of the night. A few weeks later, I found out that Kayla was pregnant and I had to change my ways. On my birthday, Kayla killed herself along with the baby. I lost everything that night that I tried to kill myself until Devon shot me. Soon after, I was in the hospital. I had nightmares about my past and you. I cut myself and not sleeping that I was sent to the mental hospital for seven years. At first I was doing bad until I met a girl named Shannon Taylor who helped me get through my tough times. By 2013, I was almost healed and I was about to be released when Shannon committed suicide. After that, I went downhill again. I was diagnosed as an insomniatic and suicidal. Until last Christmas, I woke up from a nightmare one night and I saw you sitting at my window. You told me that I needed to get better so I can see you again. You were a guardian angel to me. You protected me and took my nightmares away from me. I improved, because of you. I got out of the hospital last week and I wanted to see you right away, but your mother told me that you weren't living in Lake Park anymore and you moved to San Francisco. I had to find you so I can apologize to you for the mistakes I made to you."

"Oh my god! I can't believe that you went through all that and I let it happen. I am so sorry for letting all that happen to you." Mary blamed herself.

"No Mary, don't blame yourself for what happened to me in the last twelve years. I deserve all those things and I've changed now. Anyways, tell me what have you been up to."

"Well, after our break up a couple of months later in December, my friends took me to the winter dance where I met Daniel who became my boyfriend and my husband. We both graduated high school and attended Lake Park Community College together. Daniel majored in acting and I majored in child education. I worked at Children's Heart's Day Care Center from college and when I got married…"

"When did you get married?" Will, with shock and Mary brought out the cookies from the oven.

"I married Daniel on July 17th, 2014. It was a lovely ceremony and it was a day I will never forget. A year later, Daniel and I moved to San Francisco, California so Daniel can continue with his career. I got a job at Kinder Care until I got pregnant with Deacon, my son. After, I quit my job and became a homemaker to take care of my kids. Now, I have a daughter named Natalie and I'm living a great life."

William just stared at his coffee cup, letting all the information sink in.

"William, are you okay? Did any of this shock you?" Mary sat next to him.

"It does, but I do deserve losing you in my life. I'm just glad that you are happy with your life."

"Thanks William for understanding." Mary hugged him.

"Hey mom. I'm tired of playing outside. When can I have a cookie?" Deacon came into the house and into his mother's arms.

"Hey sweetheart, the cookies just came out of the oven. I'll give you a cookie once they cool off." Mary picked up Deacon.

"Okay mommy." Deacon smiled.

"Deacon, I want you to meet one of my old friends that I haven't seen since high school. This is my friend, William Valmont. Will, this is my son, Deacon."

"It's nice to meet you Deacon." William waved to Deacon.

"Hi."

William looked at Mary as she gave Deacon a cookie. On the outside, he was happy for Mary, but on the inside, he still loved her.

"Mare, I've gotta head back to the hotel I'm staying at. I'll come back in a few days and maybe meet your husband and daughter." William got up and headed for the front door.

"Oh okay. Deacon, stay here in the kitchen and have your snack. Why don't you come over for dinner on Thursday?" Mary walked Will to the door.

"That would be nice Mare, thank you. See you on Thursday." William hugged Mary and left.

CHAPTER TWENTY-ONE

I Still Have Feelings For You

Wednesday, July 17th, 2019, was Daniel and Mary's eighth wedding anniversary. Daniel came home the night before and planned out what they were going to do that night.

"Mary, tonight, Sarah and Jeremy are babysitting Deacon and Natalie while we go celebrate our anniversary." Daniel stopped his wife from making dinner.

"Okay, let me go upstairs and change." Mary got up from the kitchen table.

At 6:30, Daniel waited for Mary in the living room.

"Now Daniel, make sure Mary has a great time tonight." Sarah warned Daniel.

"I will Sarah. I have a lot planned for tonight. I know that she'll have a great time tonight." Daniel assured Sarah.

"Daniel, where are you? I'm ready to go." Mary came downstairs.

Daniel walked into the hall to find Mary dressed in a pink short halter dress with her hair down and straightened.

"Mary, you look so beautiful tonight." Daniel gazed at Mary.

"Thank you honey. Why don't we get going." Mary smiled at her husband.

"Oh yes, let's go."

"Have fun Mary. Don't worry about anything tonight. Just focus on your anniversary and Daniel." Sarah told Mary and held Natalie.

"I will Sarah, I will. Just take care of Deacon and Natalie." Mary kissed Natalie and walked out the door.

Daniel took Mary to the Manhattan restaurant in downtown San Francisco.

"Daniel, this place is wonderful! It has a great view of the bay from here." Mary looked outside.

"I know dear. I just want us to have the perfect anniversary tonight." Daniel held his wife's hand.

"I can't believe that I let this happen to William and I was so stupid for breaking up with him! I could've helped him through his drug and alcohol addictions." Mary stared at the table.

"Mary, Mary, are you okay?"

"Huh? Oh yeah, I'm okay." Mary snapped out of her mind and ate her dinner.

At 8:30, Daniel took Mary to Golden Gate Park for a romantic walk.

"Mary, are you sure that you are feeling okay, because you were acting weird during dinner?" Daniel touched her face.

"Of course I'm okay babe. I'm just having a great time with you on our special day together. I am so lucky to be with you Daniel Potter and I am very happy to be with you." Mary wrapped her arms around her husband.

"Thank goodness you are having fun. Come on honey, I have a surprise for you." Daniel looked into Mary's eyes and led her off the bridge next to the pond.

"Okay, what is it?"

"I brought a stereo with some of your favorite songs that we can dance to tonight right here in your favorite place." Daniel turned on the stereo.

The two danced in the park as the stars lit the ground and the water sparkled with the lights from the Golden Gate Bridge.

Mary pictured William dancing with her instead of Daniel and was happy again for the rest of the night.

On Friday, Mary hoped that William would come back and see her, but he never did. She worried about Will and wondered if he disappeared and went back to his old habits.

"Mary, babe, can you go check up on Natalie and see if she's ready to wake up?" Daniel helped his son color.

Mary didn't hear her husband. She continued to stare out the living room window.

"Sweetie? Mary! Deacon, why don't you finish coloring your picture for your mom okay." Daniel looked at Mary with concern.

"Okay dad." Deacon continued to color.

"Mary, are you all right?" Daniel walked to the living room and tapped Mary's shoulder.

"Huh? Oh, yeah. I'm all right."

"Are you sure that you are all right? I'm starting to worry about you and you are neglecting our family. You know, you can always tell me anything. You don't have to keep secrets from me. If there is anything you want to say to me then say it."

"There is nothing on my mind right now. I'm fine, I'm going to check on Natalie, okay." Mary defended herself, got up from her chair, and went upstairs.

There is something wrong with Mary. I can't let this go on any longer. I don't want to lose Mary from my life. I need to call Sarah... maybe she might know something about this." Daniel watched Mary go upstairs.

Daniel walked into the kitchen, picked up the phone, and called Sarah.

"Sarah, I need you to talk to Mary." Daniel anxiously to Sarah.

"Why? What's going on with her Dan?" Sarah, with concern.

"Ever since the night of our anniversary, Mary has been acting weird and she's been neglecting me and the kids. She maybe worried about something, but she isn't telling me anything at all and I'm getting worried about her."

"Oh man, Mary is thinking of William Valmont. If I tell Daniel the truth, it will break his heart." Sarah panicked.

"Okay Daniel, I'll come over tomorrow and I'll see if Mary can tell me what's going on." Sarah calmed Daniel down.

"Okay. Thank you so much Sarah."

Saturday afternoon, Sarah came by while Daniel worked on a movie scene at the San Francisco theater.

"Mary, Daniel called me last night saying that something is wrong and you are neglecting your family lately. Do you want to tell me if anything is bugging you?" Sarah sat next to Mary at the kitchen table.

"Sarah, the reason why I'm forgetting my family is because of William. You see, he came back to my house a couple of days ago and apologized for what happened in high school. He also told me what happened afterwards. He was still on drugs, alcohol, he was in a gang called the Brothers of Destruction, and was about to have a baby with his girlfriend committed suicide."

"Who was his girlfriend?"

"Her name was Kayla Hampshire."

"Wait a minute. Susan used to hang out with her all the time. Kayla was the popular girl and head cheerleader at our high school before she graduated. When she went away for college, she changed. She became a gang member. What I heard last time from Susan was that Kayla was having a baby and that was that. I can't believe she would kill herself."

"Yeah, but anyways, when William found her, he wanted to kill himself, but his friend Devon shot him in the arm when he tried to stop William from committing suicide. Devon took Kayla and William to the hospital and abandoned him, while. Will had nightmares about what happened after our break up that he became suicidal. His doctor sent him to Valley Lake Mental Hospital where he was there for eight years. He was diagnosed as a drug addict, an alcoholic, suicidal, and an insomniatic. William told me that last Christmas, he stopped having nightmares after he saw me in his room. I was a guardian angel to him, I protected him, I took away all of his nightmares, and I made him healthy again. He told me that he thought about me everyday and when he got out of the mental hospital, he wanted to apologize to me and he wanted to save our friendship." Mary broke into tears.

"Oh Mary." Sarah got up and hugged her friend.

"It's all my fault Sarah. It's my fault for breaking up with William and having him go through all this mess." Mary continued to cry.

"He got himself into this mess before you broke up with him Mare. So, it's basically his fault." Sarah tried to calm Mary.

"I told William that I got married and had children, I could tell that he was upset and heartbroken. That's why he didn't come on Thursday like he promised me he would. I just hope he didn't go back to his old ways again." Mary sobbed.

"Mary, do you still have feelings for William Valmont?" Sarah let go of Mary and looked at her.

"Yes Sarah… I still have feelings for William. Ever since I saw Will again, I just couldn't stop thinking about him and I wonder if he's going to come back soon." Mary wept.

"Mary, you have to think this through. Do you want to waste your marriage with Daniel and go back to William or do you want to stay with Daniel?"

"I don't know who to choose Sarah. I love Daniel and yet I still love William too." Mary honestly to Sarah, unable to make a decision.

That evening, Daniel took Deacon and Natalie to the park near their house to see the firework show while Mary stayed home in her bedroom.

"I've waited long enough. I need to go see William so I can tell him how much I still love him and how I still want to be with him." Mary got up from her bed and went into the closet.

Mary put on the same pink halter dress she wore on her wedding anniversary with silver flat shoes. She styled her hair down and quick-straightened it. She used light makeup on her face and used her berry flower lotion and perfume to make herself lovely.

Mary got into her car and drove through downtown San Francisco to get to the Baymont Inn.

"Hi, can you tell me which room is Mr. William Valmont is staying in?" Mary asked the receptionist at the front desk.

"Sure. Mr. Valmont is in room 218. Would you like a key to get into the room?"

"No, thank you though." Mary headed towards the elevators.

After the elevator stopped on the second floor, Mary walked down the hallway to look for room 218.

Meanwhile, William was in the bathroom changing when he heard knocks at the door. He opened the door to find Mary standing there.

Mary looked at William for a minute and she jumped into his arms, happy to see him.

"Oh William, I'm so glad that you are okay. I was so worried about you." Mary held onto William.

"Of course I'm all right Mare. Why do you ask?" William calmed Mary down.

"For the last few days, I've been thinking about you. I realized that I still have feelings for you. Ever since you told me what happened to you after all these years, I blamed myself for letting this all happen when I could've helped you instead of breaking up with you."

"Don't blame yourself Mary. I messed up, but I got my priorities straightened out now. You know that I always thought about you everyday. You were always with me everyday. I never stopped thinking about you Mary." William touched Mary's face and his nose touched her nose.

Mary closed the door and went back into William's open arms.

"William, I want to be with you. My marriage to Daniel was a huge mistake and I should've married you. I love you William, I've always have."

Suddenly, without thinking of Daniel, her kids, or her future, Mary kissed William on the lips.

William felt happy to have Mary kiss him as though his gangster, drug, and alcoholic past never happened and time just stood still as they broke apart.

"Oh Mary, I still love you too. I really wanted us to be together throughout all these years. I wanted to make it up to you and we have a chance. I want to be with you too Mare. I love you and I'll never stop loving you."

"Oh William!" Mary happily kissed William.

They made out as Mary took off William's shirt and they fell onto the bed. They broke apart and William looked deeply into Mary's eyes as he watched Mary take off her dress revealing a black bra and pink underpants.

William smiled and Mary pulled him in for a kiss when Gabrielle popped into his mind.

"William, you can only be Mary's friend in this mission. You can't be her boyfriend or her husband." Gabrielle warned William.

"Mary, I can't do this. I just can't." William got off of Mary and sat next to her, placing his head in his hands.

"Why? Why can't you do this?" Mary feared rejection.

"I don't want you to waste your marriage to Daniel for me. You are very happy with Daniel and I want you to stay with him and your kids. I can't be your boyfriend Mare. I need to be your friend."

"I see. You are right William. I can't waste my marriage." Mary placed her dress on in sadness.

William looked at Mary and caught her saddened face. Mary was just about to open the door when...

"Mary... wait!" William stopped Mary and grasped her hand.

Mary turned around as tears ran down her face.

"Mary, I want to be your friend just like how we were in elementary school. I promise that I will be a better friend to you than ever before. I will always be here for you whenever you are in trouble and if you need help. If anything happens to you and Daniel, I promise that I will take care of Deacon and Natalie. I want to have this friendship last and it is stronger than anything else in the world. I won't let you down Mary ever again, I promise." William held Mary's hand and touched her face.

"You really mean it William?"

"Yes, I promise Mary. No matter what happens to us." William looked into Mary's eyes truthfully and wiped her tears away.

"Okay, I'll be your friend again. Thank you for coming into my life again." Mary happily hugged Will.

"Thanks for accepting our new, repaired friendship." William held onto Mary.

Suddenly, a purple light appeared and Mary's body disappeared. A purple orb floated in the air taking Mary's place. William picked up the orb and Gabrielle came into view.

"Congratulations William. You've successfully completed the fourth mission and collected the fourth orb." Gabrielle, proudly as the hotel room disappeared into blackness.

"I can't believe I did it. I was just about to give into temptation, but your words stopped me." William looked at the glowing orb and gave it to Gabrielle.

"Are you ready for your fifth and final mission to bring Mary back to life?" Gabrielle put the orb into her dress pocket.

"Yes, I am Gabrielle." William, anxiously and happily at the same time.

"Let's go back five years where Mary is twenty-three years old where she's an author." Gabrielle described the next mission to William as a light appeared and traveled back in time.

CHAPTER TWENTY-TWO

Mary, An Author

Gabrielle and William arrived back in William's apartment except, things looked a lot different.

"Gabrielle, where are all of Mary's things?" William looked around the place.

"Well William, Mary doesn't live here."

"What? What do you mean by she doesn't live here?"

Before long, a sandy blond haired girl came out of the bathroom in a towel and walked right past William and Gabrielle, heading towards the bedroom.

"Who the hell was that?" William panicked.

"William, that's your girlfriend, Lauren Peterson. You two met at Lake Park Community College after she fell down the stairs after class in January. You guys hit it off after you took her to the hospital. This was right after you broke up with Megan Collins."

"No, no, no, this has got to be a mistake. I don't know Lauren Peterson or Megan Collins! Lauren is not my girlfriend! Mary is my girlfriend! She's the only one I want!" William with anger and confusion.

"Well William, you lost Mary as your girlfriend and now she's in New York. She's been living there for almost three years now."

"No... she can't be in New York! Why would she be living in New York instead of living here with me?" William sat on the sofa.

"Because of you William. Here, let's go back three years tight after you graduated high school ." Gabrielle took William back to 2007.

It was Saturday, September 1ˢᵗ, 2007, two weeks after Mary's birthday and she just finished her first week of her senior year of high school when you took Mary on her last date to Langston Park.

"William, are you okay? You've been acting weird since we got to the park." Mary sat down on a bench next to the pond.

"Mary... I need to talk to you about our relationship." William got up from the bench.

"What is it Will? Tell me." Mary, with concern.

"This isn't working like I thought I hoped it would go. I need to end this relationship with you." William looked at Mary with a stern look.

"What? Why?" Mary froze with shock and got up from the bench.

"We don't have a spark, that connection that we used to have together. It feels like we just faded away and we are going separate ways. It's just not working out for us."

"No William, don't say that. We can work this out babe. You'll see." Mary touched William's face and tried to reassure him.

"No Mary! It won't work. I'm sorry, but you are a waste of time and space to date! I don't love you Mare, I never did! Infact, I never liked you! I'm in love with someone else and you don't even compare to her!"

"No Will. You're lying."

"It's true Mary. It's over and I don't want to see you anymore." William gave his word to Mary.

Mary stood there heartbroken, ashamed, and in shock as tears ran down her face.

"You know what... go ahead and be with your one true love! If you want it to be like this... then this is how it will be! Goodbye William Valmont forever!" Mary said her word and walked away from William as fast as she could.

William didn't follow Mary or try to win her back. He walked back to the bench and sat down. He smiled for a few minutes and turned into guilt as the scene stopped.

"What the hell was I thinking? I lied and broke Mary's heart like I always do!" William, angry at himself.

"You lied to Mary, William, and yet deep down you still loved her. After that, you went to Lake Park Community College to study in Criminal Justice and became a detective. You stayed in Lake Park, but you never talked or see Mary. You never went to Mary's graduation like you promised her." Gabrielle took William to May 2008.

"I can't believe that William broke your heart and didn't come to your graduation to apologize!" Elisa, angrily as they waited for their familes to come out.

"I know and I've been miserable ever since the break up. I couldn't believe that Will said that I was a waste of time and space to date." Mary sadly looked at her diploma.

"I blame that William Valmont for not letting you come to the homecoming dance and the prom for breaking your heart. You know, Kelley thought you two would last and you two made a cute couple." Elisa hugged Mary and tried to cheer her up.

"You know what Elisa, I don't need William! I've waited too long for him to come back, but he'll never come back. This is my day Elisa and I can't be miserable on my graduation day. I have to be happy on this day and for the rest of my life. I need to continue writing, The Star Sisters and get it published." Mary let go of Elisa and wiped her tears away.

"You know what Mare, after my party tonight, I'll come over and we'll discuss the plans for the summer okay." Elisa looked at Mary as their families came up to them.

"Yeah, that would be great."

"Okay. I'll see you later." Elisa walked away.

Around nine' thirty that evening, Elisa stopped over at Mary's house to see her.

"So Mare, what are your plans for the summer?" Elisa sat on Mary's bed.

"Well, I was thinking of visiting my friend, Peter Stanton in New York City. I saved up enough money from my summer job last year and I want to go." Mary grabbed her safe from underneath her bed.

"What? You're leaving Lake Park?" Elisa, with shock.

"Yeah... for a while at least. I still feel the pangs of the break up and everywhere I go, there are memories of William and I... I just need to get out of here and straighten out my life before I can come home again."

"Oh man... you know what, I'll go with you! I'll invite Kaylin and Kelley to go with us." Elisa came up with an idea.

"Really? You'd come to New York with me?"

"Of course I want to go with you. You know what, we'll all move to New York! You, me, Kelley, and Kaylin!"

"That does sound like a great idea. We can all stay at Peter's place until we earn enough money to get our own apartment." Mary agreed with Elisa's idea.

"Let's call Kelley and Kaylin and see what they think of our idea. Afterwards, we can tell your parents about our plan. What do you say Mare?"

"Let's go for it Elisa. Call Kaylin and Kelley."

A half an hour later, Elisa got off the phone with Kaylin.

"Well Mary, Kelley and Kaylin will come over to my house tomorrow to talk more about the New York plan." Elisa put her cell phone away.

"What time tomorrow?"

"Around two in the afternoon." Elisa looked at Mary.

"Sounds like a good plan." Mary put her safe away underneath her bed.

"Great, I'll pick you up tomorrow around one' forty-five." Elisa smiled at Mary.

Sunday, Elisa picked up Mary after church and took her back to her house to meet up with Kelley and Kaylin.

"So, did you guys think about the New York plan?"

"Well, I thought hard about it last night and I've decided that I wanted to go with you Mare to New York." Kelley hugged Mary.

"I'm in for New York too. I really do want to go to Columbia University and go into Photography."

"Well Mare, looks like everyone is on board with going to New York. What do you say Mare? Should we tell our parents tonight?"

"Yes, I think the time is right to tell our parents about our plans." Mary smiled at her friends.

"We'll tell our parents when we get home and we'll call each other after we break the news."

*That evening, Mary got home and waited til dinnertime to tell her parents
the news.*

*"Mom, dad, I have some news to tell you." Mary passed the corn to
Andrew.*

"What's the news dear?"

*"Well, ever since I graduated high school, I decided that I want to go to
New York with Kelley, Elisa, and Kaylin. We'll all stay at Peter's place until
we find a place we can all live together. Mom, dad, I really want to go to New
York University so I can go into the Writer's program, study writing, and find
success in New York than here. Can I please follow my dreams and let me go
to New York?"*

*"Oh Mary, of course you can go to New York with your friends. Just make
sure that you don't lose contact with us."*

*"Don't worry mom, I won't. I'll call home every few days. I better call Elisa
and tell her everything!" Mary, with happiness as she got up from the table as
the scene stopped.*

"A few days later, Mary and her friends caught a flight to New York
to start their lives in a brand new place together."

"So Mary went to New York while I stayed here and I went to
college to be a detective. I thought I was suppost to get myself into
trouble in this mission?" William, with a puzzled look on his face.

"No, you don't get into trouble in this mission Will. You just go
through numerous relationships and you don't find happiness." Gabrielle
went back to William's apartment.

"Oh great, I'm just a lonely desperate detective! Thanks Gabrielle."
William, ashamed and embarrassed.

"I'm sorry Will, but you wanted to be like this and this is where
I leave you. I'll see you when you get to New York." Gabrielle
disappeared.

Meanwhile in Manhattan's Union Square area, Mary unpacked her
things in her room that she shares with Kelley when Peter came into
the room.

"Hey, how are you doing?"

"I'm doing good. Just unloading my last set of clothes. You know Peter, I'm so happy to be here in this city. I feel like I'm starting all over with a clean slate and everything from the past year just melted away." Mary put her clothes away in her dresser.

"Good. I'm glad you like it here. What are your plans now that you are in New York City?"

"Well, tomorrow I'm going to New York University and register. They offer a great writing program for authors who want to be successful and I want to join." Mary showed Peter the NYU brochure of the Writer's Program.

"Looks like you got school planned out as well as the start of your writing career." Peter, happily put his arm around Mary.

"I'm almost done writing, The Star Sisters. During my first semester, I'll show my teachers my book and see what they think." Mary showed Peter her story.

Peter read The Star Sisters and was amazed by Mary's writing.

"Wow Mare… this is a fascinating story. You really know how to write."

"Thanks. I'm glad you like the story Pete. I worked hard on The Star Sisters for almost two years now and I'm very happy that I'm almost done editing it." Mary happily to her friend.

"I'm not kidding. I want you to keep writing. Don't ever stop Mary. Don't let anyone or anything stop you from becoming a writer. You have an amazing gift here Mary."

"Don't worry Peter, I won't stop writing. I promise you that."

CHAPTER TWENTY-THREE

An Old Friend

Throughout the summer, Kaylin, Kelley, Elisa, and Mary got jobs to pay their share of rent to Peter.

Kaylin found a job at Upper East Video Hut in the Theater District. She registered at Columbia University in late June.

Elisa found a job at Life's Expectations Fashion Boutique on the border of Chelsea. She enrolled in New York University in July. She took her regular classes before going into the fashion designer major.

Kelley found a job as a grocery store clerk at Conston Groceries not too far from Peter's apartment. She registered at Empire State University to go straight into the Culinary Arts program.

Mary found a job as a waitress at a coffee place in Chelsea called, Carlotta's Coffee Café. She registered at New York University the same time with Elisa to enroll into the Writer's Program.

By April in 2009, the girls saved enough money to buy an apartment over in Chelsea.

It was a Wednesday afternoon, Mary came home to find Elisa on the phone with her boyfriend, Kevin Anderson.

'Babe, I'm coming home over Easter weekend to visit you and my family. We got the apartment in Chelsea. Mary just paid the final payment for the apartment today so we are set. It will be you, me, Mary, and Kaylin. Kelley is going to stay and live with Peter since they've been going out for three months now. Okay, just do your homework and I'll be there in a few days. I love you Kevin. Bye." Elisa hung up her cell phone.

"Hey Liz, I paid the final payment to Mrs. Chapman. How's Kevin holding up?" Mary put down her bag.

"Well, he's really anxious to come to NYC in the next few months once we settle in our apartment and he's happy that I'm coming home within a few days. Hey, how did Professor Stevens like your story?" Elisa sat on the couch next to her.

"Well Professor Stevens took my story home since she didn't get a chance to look at it during class. I hope she likes it." Mary, anxious about her story.

"Don't worry about it Mare. Your professor will love The Star Sisters. Your stories are special Mare and they will touch others especially Professor Stevens. Trust me. Goodness, it's almost four. I have to get ready for work. Hey, we'll talk more later, okay Mare." Elisa put her arm around her friend.

"Sure. Thanks Liz. Have a good day at work."

Thursday morning at New York University, Mary waited outside room 27A for Professor Stevens.

"Good morning Miss Radcliffe. How are you this morning?" Professor Stevens unlocked the door.

"I'm doing good. Um, Professor Stevens, did you read my story last night?" Mary asked her professor as they entered the classroom.

"Yes I did Miss Radcliffe. Your story is a hit! I loved every detail of how Bree Clarkson tells her story of her family's problems and how her four friends come to her for aid. If this story was an assignment, I would give you an A+ off the bat. However, I'm going to give you some options for the story. See me after class so I can give you the options." Professor Stevens sat behind her desk.

Mary sat through Fiction Writing class worried about the options that her professor had in store for her story. As soon as the dismissal bell rang, Mary walked up to Professor Stevens's desk.

"Did you wanted to see me Professor?"

"Yes, Miss Radcliffe. Here, I want you to have this." Professor Stevens gave Mary a folded piece of paper.

Mary opened the paper and found three publishing companies.

"Thank you so much Professor. This will help me with my writing career!" Mary thanked Professor Stevens.

"No problem Miss Radcliffe. Just keep on with your dreams and never give up. Here'a your story and I'll see you tomorrow." Professor Stevens walked out of the classroom.

Three O' clock rolled around, Mary walked off the university campus and headed home. Mary looked at the list over and over as she walked home.

As Mary walked down the Theater District, Mary bumped into a guy with dark brown hair, blue eyes, and glasses.

"Oh my gosh, I am so sorry! I wasn't watching where I was going." Mary apologized to the guy.

"No its okay. People make mistakes. Wait a minute... Are you Mary Radcliffe?" The guy looked at Mary.

"Yes I am. Do I know you?" Mary looked at the guy.

"You don't remember an old friend from high school? Its me Mare, Harry Jordan!" Harry tried to get Mary to remember him.

"Harry, oh my gosh! You've changed! How have you been? What are you doing here in NYC?" Mary hugged him.

"I've been good. Just balancing college and work. Remember back in our Senior year of high school and I sent in my application to New York University?"

"Yeah, I remember. You sent that application in November."

"I got my acceptance letter at the end of April. After graduation, I moved to New York to attend NYU."

"Wow, that's great Harry. I'm glad that you got into NYU."

"Thanks. I might be able to take classes in the Medical program next year. I really want to be a Pediatrician in the future since I love working with kids and being a doctor. So, what have you been up to after high school?"

"I wish I could talk more Harry, but my apartment is coming up." Mary said as they walked onto North State Street.

"Oh, well… um… Do you want to get together after class and catch up some more?" Harry stopped at the Theater apartment building.

"Sure. I get out of computer class around three. That would be perfect."

"Great. I'll meet you at the Chelsea Café on State Street in Union Square at three' fifteen tomorrow."

"Cool. I'll see you then." Mary entered the building.

"What? You saw Harry Jordan today! How is he?" Kaylin with shock.

"Harry is doing fine. He is going to the same college as I am attending. He's studying to be a Pediatrician and he's living in this city!"

"Really that's nice! Did you tell Harry that you are going to the same school as he is?"

"No, not yet, but I am going to meet up with Harry tomorrow at the Chelsea Café after school." Mary, with excitement.

"Nice. So… are you going to go out with Harry or take it slow with him first?" Kaylin, with curiosity.

"I don't know yet Kay. I want to get to know Harry again before I go out with him." Mary blushed.

"Oh come on Mare, you need to start dating again. It's been two years since you've had a boyfriend and it's time that you had one." Kaylin scolded.

"Yea, you're right Kaylin. It's been two years. Maybe I should go out with Harry. First, I'll reconnect with Harry before I get into a relationship with him. Besides, it's my fault for disconnecting my close friendship with Harry in the first place after September. I do like Harry a lot, but I really want to take it slow with Harry and not screw this up."

Friday afternoon…

"Remember class that your internet research paper is due Monday. It is required to be typed! Class dismissed." Professor Coleman told the class.

Mary headed out of the university doors and walked onto West Seventy-seventh Street and headed to Union Square.

Harry waited for Mary at the Chelsea Café when he spotted her walking down the street.

"Hey Mare, how are you?" Harry got up from the table and hugged Mary.

"I'm fine. I just got out of class not too long ago." Mary let go of each other and sat down at a table by the window.

"What college are you going to Mare?"

"I'm attending NYU, Har. The same school that you are going to."

"That's great! When did you start at NYU?"

"I started at the end of August. I signed up for my general classes last year and I signed up for the Writer's Program to advance my writing career. This year, my Fiction Writing professor gave me a list of three publishing companies here in the city for my book, The Star Sisters. I'm going to check out the companies this weekend. My professor loved my writing that she told me to stick to it and never give up on writing."

"That's great Mare. I'm happy for you. How come you are here in New York City? I thought you were going to still stay in Lake Park with your boyfriend. Um... What's his name? Uh... William Valmont?" Harry with concern.

"Well Harry... William broke up with me for another girl after senior year started. I never told you that, because I couldn't talk about it. After graduation, I moved to New York to get away from the horrible memories. I came with, Elisa Collins, Kaylin Robinson, and Kelley Brooks here and we are living with my ex-boyfriend Peter Stanton. When school is over, Liz, Kaylin, and I are moving into our new apartment in Chelsea."

"Oh man, I am so sorry that he broke your heart. If I was with you, I would never break your heart." Harry took Mary's hand and held it.

"Really, thanks Harry. I pretty much gotten over the break up and just stuck with writing." Mary looked into Harry's eyes.

"You know what, I'll go with you to check out the publishing companies over the weekend if you like the idea."

"That would be great Harry. I'm starting tomorrow at one so you can just stop at my place before we go. Thank you so much Harry."

"No problem Mare. I'd do anything for you." Harry continued to hold Mary's hand and looked into her eyes.

"I know that Mary has been through a lot over these two years, but I'm going to stand by Mary's side tomorrow at the publishing companies and from now on."

Saturday afternoon, Harry met up with Mary at her place before setting out to Ziff Davis Publishing Company.

"Hey Mare, you ready to go?"

"Yep. I've got my manuscript right here in my bag."

"Cool. Let's go catch a cab and head over to 63 Madison Avenue right away." Mary locked the apartment.

It was two in the afternoon when Harry and Mary walked out of the Ziff Davis building.

"I can't believe that Ziff Davis turned your story down." Harry, with disappointment and held the door open for Mary.

"I know, but I need to get used to rejection Harry if I want to continue with my writing career. At least we got two more publishing companies left to try." Mary, with no worry.

"Where do you want to try next?"

"Let's try Daw Books in Downtown next." Mary read the list.

"Okay, Taxi!"

Two hours past, Mary and Harry sat in Mrs. Jane Huberman's office.

"Ms. Radcliffe, this is a very interesting story. I love ever detail that you put into the story and it captures my imagination. I would love to publish your story."

"Really? Are you serious?" Mary, with shock.

"Yes. You have an amazing gift here Mary and I'm going to help you accomplish your dream. Why don't we set up an appointment on Tuesday at four' thirty in the afternoon and we'll set a date on your book's release and the profit you will get."

"Thank you Mrs. Huberman! Thank you so much for helping me take my dream another step further!" Mary shook Mrs. Huberman's hand.

After they got out of the Daw Books building, Mary and Harry went to Central Park to celebrate.

"I can't believe that my book is going to be published! My dreams are finally coming true!" Mary hugged Harry.

"Mary, I am so proud of you accomplishing your dreams! You are going to be a fantastic writer Mary." Harry held onto Mary.

"Thank you Harry, for supporting me through this whole thing. I really appreciate it." Mary let go of Harry and looked into his eyes.

"Mary, can I ask you why did William break up with you two years ago?" Harry sat with Mary on a bench near the lake.

"Harry... William didn't break up with me, he dumped me for another girl who supposedly was his true love. He also told me that he never liked me, we faded away, and I was a waste of time and space to date."

"Oh man, that's a horrible thing to say! Man, and I thought that William Valmont was a nice guy. He always treated you right and showed you respect and yet..." Harry began.

"And he used me Harry! William played me throughout the years. After I helped him get out of trouble, he gets back into trouble." Mary, sadly.

"Mary, it was William's fault for breaking your heart and stealing your innocence. You are better off without him now that everything is happening for you."

"I know. Thank you."

Without thinking it, Harry touched Mary's face and kissed her lovingly on her lips.

Harry broke apart from Mary and smiled at her. Mary smiled back at Harry and put her arms around Harry.

"Do you still want to walk around the park or do you want to stay here?" Harry stroked Mary's hair.

"Actually, I would like to stay here for a while. It's nice here by the lake and by you." Mary fell asleep in Harry's arms.

MARY ROZA

In early June, Mary, Kaylin, and Elisa moved out of Peter's apartment and into the apartment on Park Grove Avenue in Chelsea. Two weeks later, <u>The Star Sisters</u> released into stores around the United States.

"Mary, I just picked up a copy of your book and it was the last copy on the shelves!"

"What? Are you serious? I never expected my book would be popular this quickly!" Mary suddenly looked at Kaylin.

"Well, I think you better start on book number two Mare. If people like the first Star Sisters book, they are bound to like the second book." Kaylin advised Mary.

"I will Kaylin. I'll see what I can come up with later on tonight."

In June of 2011, Mary graduated out of the Writing program at NYU. Harry started his internship at Bellevue Hospital while he took classes in the medical field.

Mary started writing, <u>The Star Sisters: Love Comes to the Sisters</u> during the summer. She completed the first draft of the book in the spring of 2012.

"So, when are you going to send your second book into Mrs. Huberman?"

"Probably this fall in November. I'm kind of scared of sending the story in." Mary turned her laptop on.

"Why?" Harry sat up on the bed.

"I think that the second book won't be as good as the first book." Mary looked at the script.

"That's crazy Mary! Your second book will be as good as the first book. The first Star Sisters made the Best Seller's list topping number one just three weeks after it came out." Harry reminded Mary of last year.

"You're right Harry. I shouldn't be worried about the second book. It doesn't matter how people like my books, its how the writing and creativity of my books make it count."

"That's the spirit Mare. Are you going to write more books on the Star Sisters?"

"I am going to write a third book and afterwards, I'm going to take a break from the Star Sisters for a while and write something else." Mary laid out her plans for her career.

"Cool. Hey, are we still on for the Maroon 5 concert in Central Park tonight?"

"Yes, we are still on for the concert tonight. We can stop by the Corner Café by the park, grab something to eat, and head to the concert afterwards."

"Sounds like a good plan Mary. I'll pick you up at seven. I better get to the hospital. I got a short shift today." Harry hugged Mary.

"All right. See you tonight. Have fun at work."

By the time December came, Mary's second book was out in stores and it rocketed to number one on the Best Seller's list putting the first book in second place.

"Mary, did you read the Entertainment Weekly about your second book?"

"No why?"

"Your second book made it to number one on the chart!" Kaylin showed Mary the magazine.

"What? Oh my god, I'm number one again!" Mary looked at the magazine in shock.

"Congratulations Mare. Your writing career is really sky rocketing!" Elisa put her arm around her friend.

"Thanks Liz. You know, I've been hearing that you and Kevin talking lately about getting your own apartment when you guys graduate. Well, I want to help you guys out." Mary looked at Elisa.

"Really Mare? You are going to help me and Kevin out?"

"Yes, since you helped me escape from Lake Park, I want to return the favor and help you find an apartment." Mary made a promise to Elisa.

"Thank you Mary! Thank you!" Elisa happily got up and hugged Mary.

"It's no problem Liz. Life for me is getting better and better for me and I couldn't be more happier in New York right now." Mary smiled and looked out the frosty window.

Meanwhile back in Lake Park, William tried to enjoy his life, but he couldn't. He was a detective for the Lake Park Police Department for two years now. He lived in an apartment on Rosemont Road and juggled relationships with women.

It was around eight' thirty in the morning, Will looked at the ceiling in misery.

"Hey baby, good morning." Lauren rolled over and placed her arms around William.

"Hey hon, I'm okay. Just enjoying this morning lying right next to you." William lied to his girl as he held her.

"You know what, I'm going to make breakfast while you just stay here and wait for me." Lauren kissed William's cheek, got up, and left the room.

William sat up in bed and put on his black pants. He walked over to the window and looked over at Langston Park. Will remembered the dreams of Mary. The dreams were all flashbacks of Mary and him in high school before their break up.

"Why am I not happy? I have a great job, a nice place to live in, and a girlfriend. Why do I feel so horrible inside me?"

After a few minutes of thinking, he found the solution.

"Oh man, I'm still in love with Mary Radcliffe even though I dumped her six years ago. I dream about her almost every night and I try to ignore them, but I just can't get her out of my head! I wonder where she is at and what she's doing over the years."

"Sweetie, breakfast is ready!" Lauren brought in a tray of food into the room.

"Babe, I'm sorry, but I'm going to skip breakfast and go to work early. I need to finish up on a difficult case. I'll see you later. Love you." William kissed Lauren.

"Oh, could you do me a favor? Could you do me a favor? Could you get me the new Star Sisters book by Mary Radcliffe?" Lauren sat on the bed.

"Sure I will. I'll stop at the bookstore on my way home from work. I better get ready. See you." William headed to the bathroom.

At Books in Midnight bookstore an hour later, William picked up a copy of <u>The Star Sisters: Love Comes to the Sisters</u>.

Secretly, William read the first Star Sisters book and he thought the book was very good.

He opened the back part of the book to find Mary's picture on the flap side of the cover.

"Oh Mary... It seems like you never change. You are happier now that I'm not in your life." William stared at Mary's picture.

William closed the book, paid it up front, and left the bookstore.

At the Lake Park Police Department, William worked on a case report when Noah Washell came by.

"Hey Will, you're here early today." Noah, with surprise.

"Yeah, I needed to get out of my place for a while." Will grabbed his coffee cup and headed to the lounge.

"Is it Lauren?" Noah closed the lounge door.

"No actually. It's Mary. I've been dreaming about her for the last couple of weeks maybe longer than that and I've been thinking about her lately." William poured himself some coffee.

"What? Oh my god! Are you still in love with Mary Radcliffe?"

"Yes Noah, I still love her even though I broke her heart years ago for nothing. I didn't mean to hurt her, I wanted to love her. I don't love Lauren and I didn't love Megan either. I only love Mary!"

"Wow, I can't believe you lied to my best friend all along and you screwed yourself with meaningless relationships."

"I know, I am so stupid! I need to find Mary and apologize to her." William sat down and put his face in his hands.

"Well good luck trying to find her in this town." Noah drank his coffee.

"Why do you say that Noah?" William, with confusion.

"Because Mary left town right after graduation."

"What?" William looked up.

"Yeah. Susan told me that Mary left, because she couldn't take the pangs of the break up and the memories of you that she took off to New York with Elisa, Kelley, and Kaylin. Since then, Mary never came back to Lake Park."

"That means that I have to go to New York to win Mary back."

"Yep and I suggest you do that the minute you get home or go in the spring when it gets warmer. It's up to you."

"I'm going to go to New York in April, but I have to tell all of this to Lauren tonight when I get home."

"Yep, but you better act fast before Mary moves on with her life."

Six that evening, William came home to find Lauren in the kitchen making dinner.

"Hey honey, how was work?" Lauren hugged and kissed William.

"It was all right. Um Lauren, we need to talk about us." William took Lauren's hand and led her to the living room.

"Look, I know that we have been going out for six months now and we've been a great couple, but there is someone else that I love. I loved her ever since I laid eyes on her. I need to find Mary Radcliffe and apologize to her for the mistakes I made, but the only thing that's holding me back is you. I'm sorry, but I need to break up with you Lauren."

"Wait a minute, you went out with Mary Radcliffe before she became a writer? I can't believe that you didn't tell me! Why did you break up with her?" Lauren questioned William.

"I lied to her. I told her that I didn't love her and there was another girl I loved."

"You lied to her! How could you do that to her? What the hell was wrong with you?"

"I don't know why I broke up with Mary. I was selfish and greedy to Mary. I need to go to New York, confess my love to her, and win her back."

"I don't know why you broke up with Mary in the first place. You know, you are right. We have been fizzling for the last three weeks. Mary deserves to be with you. Go find her and win her back."

"Thank you Lauren. I better start getting everything together before I leave for New York in the spring." William hugged Lauren, got up, and went into his room.

CHAPTER TWENTY-FOUR

Searching For Mary

"Thanks Lauren for helping me plan this out and being my friend." William hugged Lauren.

"No problem. We are friends and I'll be here whenever you need help. Now, get your butt on that plane and win Mary's heart back!"

"Okay, I'm going. Do you have everything under control here?"

"Yes I do. You have three weeks to win Mary back. By the time you come back, I'll be out of your apartment."

"Okay thank you Lauren. I owe you for this. I'll see you when I get back." William turned and walked through the terminal.

It was around one' forty-five when William arrived in the Manhattan area. He checked himself into the Ritz Hotel and didn't know where to start.

"I see you make it to New York in one piece." Gabrielle walked around the room.

"Yes, I broke up with Lauren, came to New York, and now I am trying to find a location where I can start looking for Mary." William panicked.

"William, think back to high school, a few days after you started your senior year and Mary started her junior year." Gabrielle gave William an idea.

Will remembered on Friday night in late September of 2006. He was at Mary's house hanging out with her and studying together.

"Hey babe, what's this letter from?" William looked at the envelope.

"Oh, it's from my ex-boyfriend, Peter Stanton. Remember, Peter and I dated during my freshman and half of sophomore year? We broke up after second semester since we drifted a lot over winter break." Mary told her boyfriend the story.

"Oh yeah, I remember him. You guys are just friends now, right?" William with worry.

"Of course we are just friends. Peter and I are like brother and sister to each other. You don't need to worry. He wrote me saying that he moved to New York to attend Columbia University to start his music career. He says that he loves New York and that I should visit him sometime." Mary read the letter.

"That's it! Peter Stanton. I'll start my search at Peter's place." William snapped out of his memory.

"Good start Will. Here's the address. I hope you do find Mary soon before something happens."

William didn't worry about Gabrielle's words that he walked out of his room and caught a cab to start his search.

In Union Square at four' fifteen, William was on North State Street walking into the Theater apartment building and looked at the directory. Peter's apartment was on the second floor, room 205. William rang the doorbell and Kelley answered the door.

"Hi, is Peter there?"

"Yeah, he is. Let me go call him. Hon, there is someone asking for you at the door."

"What is it sweetie? Oh, um, Kelley, can I have a few minutes with one of my friends?" Peter, in shock after he saw William at the door.

"Yeah sure. I'll get back to my homework." Kelley walked into the kitchen.

"William, what the hell are you doing here?" Peter closed the door.

"Look Peter, I'm here to win Mary back. I was wrong to break Mary's heart. I love her and I can't be without her. Can I please go in and talk to her?" William begged Peter.

"I'm sorry Will, but Mary doesn't live here anymore."

"What? Where is she then?" William panicked.

"Look, if I tell you where Mary is at now, she'll never forgive me for that." Peter seriously to William.

"Just tell me where she is Pete. I really need to see Mary again and tell her how much I love her. Please, I need to know!" William begged Peter.

"Okay, I'll tell you where Mary is at. She moved out with her friends, Elisa and Kaylin and found an apartment on Park Grove Avenue in Chelsea. Here's the address." Peter told William everything.

"Thank you Peter. Thank you so much for helping me find Mary." William took the piece of paper.

"It's no problem. Now go find Mary."

"I will. Thanks a lot." William walked away.

After getting out of Union Square, William went to Central Park before heading to Chelsea.

"All right, I need to apologize to Mary first before I ask her out again. I don't think I'll be able to see her today. I might go see her tomorrow, but I'd better go see what her apartment looks like first." Will walked out of the park and headed to Chelsea.

Around five' ten, Mary was in her room working on the final draft of The Star Sisters Three: Destinies of the Star Sisters.

"Mare, Kaylin's making dinner tonight. It will be done soon." Elisa walked into Mary's room.

"Great, thanks Elisa."

"You almost done with your book, Mare?" Elisa sat on Mary's bed.

"Yeah, I'm going to send it to Mrs. Huberman tomorrow and see what she thinks of the story." Mary got up from her desk and looked out her window.

"That's good Mary. Is there a fourth book running through your head right now?"

"I don't know Elisa. I was thinking of taking a break from the Star Sisters and write a book on something else. I might just take a break for a..." Mary suddenly stopped talking.

Mary gazed over towards Chelsea Park and spotted a familiar face.

"Mary, are you okay? Why did you stop talking all of a sudden?"

"Elisa, I think William Valmont found me!"

"What? No way Mare. He doesn't know where you are and its been six years since you spoken or even seen him. It's probably a guy who looks like him that's all." Elisa looked out the window.

"Yeah I guess you are right. Come on, let's go eat." Mary ignored her fear and left the room with Elisa.

Sunday afternoon around three' fifteen, Mary went to Daw Books to drop off her book. Elisa spent the whole day with Kevin in the city and Kaylin was at work until eleven.

"Here you go Jane, my third installment for the Star Sisters." Mary gave her finished copy to Mrs. Huberman.

"Thank you Mary. Now, are you going to take a break from writing a little bit?"

"Yes I am. Just only for a little while until I can get some new ideas for a story."

"That's good Mare. You just take your time okay. Call me if you have a new story that you want published." Mrs. Huberman walked Mary to the door.

"I will Jane, thank you. Have a great Sunday." Mary walked to the elevator.

"You too Mary, bye." Mrs. Huberman walked back into her office.

Mary decided to walk back to her apartment since it was a beautiful day outside.

She was just about to go inside the complex building when she heard,

"Mary! Mary!"

Mary turned around to see William Valmont walking across the street towards her.

"No, it can't be William! This has got to be a dream. It has to be!" Mary panicked, closed her eyes, and opened them every few minutes.

Every time Mary did it, she still see William walking towards her.

"Hello Mary. Its been awhile." William smiled.

"What are you doing here Will? How in the world did you find me?"

"Your old friend Noah Washell told me that you moved to New York and Peter Stanton told me where you were living at now. Mary, I need to talk to you about what happened six years ago when I dumped you."

"I don't think that I want to talk to you about what happened six years ago or even you right now." Mary walked away from William.

"What? Wait a minute Mare. Please, just let me explain myself. Look, I know that I broke your heart and I left you angry and abandoned, but I didn't mean for it to happen. I never meant to hurt you." William chased Mary into Central Park.

"Look Will, you're not sorry for hurting me at all! You just used me for your own games!"

"I never used you at all! I never did. I loved you Mary and I never stopped loving you."

"No, you didn't! Look, my life has gotten better and better since you walked out of my life six years ago! You need to stay away from me and leave me alone!" Mary snapped at William and they stopped on a hill near the deep pond.

Suddenly, a piece of the ground crumbled as Mary lost her balance and fell down the hill.

Mary rolled down to the deep pond, hit her head on the rock, and landed in the water.

William ran down the hill and jumped into the pond as Mary sunk into the water. He found Mary at the bottom of the pond, scooped her in his arms, and swam back to the surface.

He pulled Mary to a soft spot next to the pond and began to do CPR on her.

"Come on Mary, I know that you are still in there just don't be dead."

Mary coughed up water and William turned her to her side to breathe.

"Will? Why did you save me?"

"I saved you Mary, because I love you and I don't want to lose you again. Here, let me help you up. How are you feeling?" William helped Mary up.

"I'm okay, but I feel a little dizzy." Mary felt her head.

"You hit your head and you're bleeding a little bit. Let's go back to your apartment and get you cleaned and dried up."

"William, why did you save me?" Mary asked William as he cleaned the cuts on her face.

"I saved your life Mary, because I love you." Will put the washcloth back into the bowl.

"Then, why did you break up with me if you loved me in the first place!" Mary looked into William's eyes.

"I don't know what was going through my head that day. I was stubborn, stupid, selfish, and thoughtless. I always had feelings for you Mary. After you left the park and the days after, I went through difficult relationships with women and I was unhappy. I kept on thinking about you everyday and how miserable you were without me at your side. I was so stupid for breaking your heart and I'm never going to do that to you ever again. I just want to be with you and have another chance with you." William touched Mary's face.

"Oh William, there's something I need to tell you too. The truth is that I still love you and I missed you over the years. I only wanted to be with you and no body else. When you crushed my heart, I couldn't move on in my life. I thought I was doing something wrong in our relationship and it was all my fault for losing you." Mary cried.

"No Mary, its not your fault. It was my fault for leaving you."

"I know, I know. I just want to be your girlfriend again and I'll try to be perfect for you." Mary cheered up.

"Mary, you were always perfect to me." William wrapped his arms around Mary's waist and leaned towards her for a kiss.

Before William touched Mary's lips with his lips, the doorbell rang.

"Hold on Will. Let me go get the door. I'll be right back." Mary placed on her light pink robe and walked out of the room.

Mary answered the door to find Harry there with two pink roses.

"Mary, I know that we've been friends since sixth grade, but there is something that I need to tell you." Harry walked into the living room.

"What is it Harry? You can tell me." Mary went up to Harry.

"Mary, I have feelings for you ever since senior year of high school. I wanted to ask you out so many times, but I always chicken out. I know that I'm going out with Karen Marshall, but I want to be with you, Mare. Oh my god, what happened to you and why is your hair all wet?" Harry looked at Mary's face.

"Oh, after I dropped off my book, I went to the park, I fell down the hill into the deep pond, and William saved my life."

"William, William Valmont found you here in New York!"

"Yes he did. He apologized to me and saved my life from drowning."

"Are you going to go back out with William?"

"I don't know Har. I mean, William told his feelings for me and he was sorry for ever breaking my heart. I only love William the most in my life. I always loved William Valmont, Harry. I know you have feelings for me, but I only like you as a friend Harry."

"I understand Mary. I can tell that you are in love with William. I'll stay with Karen, because I love her as much as you love Will."

"You should Harry. You two make a great couple together."

"Yeah, you're right. I better head over to Karen's place and give her the roses. Good luck with William. Just remember, that I will always be here for you no matter what happens. I'll call you later. See you." Harry hugged Mary and left.

"Bye Harry." Mary got up from the couch.

After the door closed, Mary went back to her room to find William on her bed waiting for her.

"Is everything okay?" William sat up.

"Yeah, everything is fine. One of my friends decided to stop by for a little bit. He needed some advice from me and left." Mary sat on Will's lap.

"Oh, that's good." William looked at Mary.

They both looked at each other deeply for a few minutes.

William couldn't take it anymore that he grew closer to Mary and kissed her, longing for her. They both fell back to the pillows and made out.

"Wait a minute, are you sure that you want to do this?" Mary, anxiously as Will tried to take off her robe.

"I do Mare. I figured out who I want to be with and I want to be with you and only you. I know I messed up before by losing you to my selfishness, but I don't want to lose you again. I assure you that I am never going to leave you again. I'm not like that anymore. Nothing bad is going to come between us anymore. I promise you, Mary. I'm going to love you better than before. You are the one for me, Mare. I'm being completely honest with you. No more lies!" William touched Mary's face.

"Oh William!" Mary let Will kiss her.

Will took off Mary's robe and kissed every part of her body. Mary took off William's shirt and pants.

"Are you sure Mary?" Will stopped for a minute.

"Yes, I'm sure. I love you William and I don't want us to end." Mary wrapped her arms around William.

William looked at Mary for a couple of seconds and kissed her again.

Around seven' thirty, William woke up to find a sleeping Mary in his arms.

"Mary, are you okay?" William whispered to Mary as she stirred.

"Yes, I am. You just wore me out." Mary held onto Will.

"Mary, will you be my girlfriend again?" William stroked Mary's hair.

"Yes, I will be your girl again William." Mary smiled and stroked his hair.

"I love you Mary Radcliffe." William kissed Mary.

CHAPTER TWENTY- FIVE

A Love Reunited

At nine, Mary and William watched TV when Elisa and Kevin came home.

"Hey Mary, what's he doing here?"

"Kevin, Liz, I have wonderful news. William Valmont came to New York and apologized to me for breaking my heart."

"Is this true William?"

"Yes it's true Liz. I realized that I only love Mary. I never wanted to hurt her in the first place. I sacrificed everything to come to New York, find Mary, and declare my love to her again. I promise you guys that I will never hurt Mary in any way again."

"All right William, you better not break my best friend's heart again otherwise, Kevin will take care of you!" Elisa warned William.

"I promise you Liz, that I will love Mary always and forever more. She is the only girl I want and no one else." William told Elisa and held Mary's hand.

"Well, you have my blessings to be with Mary." Elisa hugged William.

"Thank you Liz. Can William stay with us since he's staying at a hotel?"

"Sure, he can stay here Mare for as long as he wants to."

"Thank you Elisa. Come on babe, let's go get your stuff from the Ritz Hotel." Mary looked at William.

Weeks past, Elisa and Kevin moved out of the apartment and moved to West Village.

"I can't believe that you and William are back together after all the things he put you through." Kaylin sat next to Mary in the living room.

"I know, I've just been so much happier now these days since William came back into my life."

"I'm glad that you and Will are back together. I always knew that you two would last." Kaylin, happily to her friend.

"Thanks Kay. All of my dreams came true for me. I'm a successful writer, I live in New York, and I have a great boyfriend, but there is something missing." Mary turned from happy to sad.

"What's the matter Mare?" Kaylin, with concern.

"Well, I think that William is getting homesick. He misses his work back in Lake Park. I'm also getting homesick too. I haven't been home in the longest time and if William goes back alone, the relationship won't last." Mary got worried.

"Then you have to choose Mary. Either you go back to Lake Park with your boyfriend or stay in New York."

"Its not that simple Kay. I can't make a decision yet."

"Then you need to talk to William about this situation and maybe you two will come up with a solution to this problem."

"I guess you are right Kaylin. I'll talk to Will after dinner about this."

After dinner, Mary walked into her room to find William with one of her books.

"Babe, I've gotta say, you have a gift in writing. I always knew you did." William put down the first book of the Star Sisters and walked over to his girlfriend.

"Yeah, I am blessed to have this gift in writing." Mary sadly hugged her boyfriend.

"Hon, are you okay? What's the matter?" William looked at Mary's face.

"William... um... are you happy here in New York with me?" Mary studdered.

"Of course I am happy to be here with you, but my vacation time is almost over and soon I'll have to go back to Lake Park."

"I knew this was going to happen. You are going to go home and we'll go through a troubled long distant relationship that won't last." Mary sat at her desk.

"Mary, that's never going to happen. I'm not going to leave you again. I'm not homesick. I have to get back to my job in Lake Park. I think the question is, are you homesick Mary?" William reassured Mary.

"Okay fine. I'm the one that is homesick. I miss Lake Park and if you go back, I'll fall apart! William, I want to go back home to Lake Park with you!"

"But what about your writing career Mare? The publishing company is here in New York. You'll be nothing without them."

"You know that I can mail my stories to Jane or I can send them off to the office in Chicago. I have plenty of other options hon. You don't have to worry." Mary reassured William.

"Are you sure that you want to go back to Lake Park?"

"Yes, I do want to go home with you babe." Mary wrapped her arms around Will's neck.

"I love you Mary. I promise you that once we get back home, We'll start our family. I promise." William touched Mary's face.

"Really? We can settle down at last?"

"Of course we can. I'm ready to settle down with you. You would make a wonderful wife to me. You are the one for me. I love you Mary Radcliffe." William kissed Mary's forehead.

"I love you too William Valmont." Mary leaned towards Will and kissed him.

Suddenly, Mary's body disappeared and a pink orb appeared on the ground. William picked up the orb and Gabrielle appeared.

"Congratulations William, your last mission is complete!" Gabrielle happily to Will.

"I know. I can't believe that I completed these five missions. Now, I can finally bring Mary back to life." William happily looked at the orb.

"Yes, it is time to bring Mary Radcliffe back to life." Gabrielle took the orb from William.

CHAPTER TWENTY-SIX

Reunited

Gabrielle took William back to the present time Lake Park. They arrived at Rose Hill Cemetery in front of Mary's tombstone. Will fell to the ground and touched the stone.

"Don't worry Mare, it won't be like this. We'll be together soon and I'll be better to you than ever before." William looked at the tombstone.

"Are you ready William?" Gabrielle touched Will's shoulder.

"Yes, I am." William moved away from the tombstone.

Gabrielle took out the five orbs from her dress pocket and gave them to Will.

"Take the orbs and place them in a circle on Mary's grave."

After William placed the pink orb onto the dirt, the orbs glowed their colors and rose up into the air.

William was amazed to see the orbs dance around with Mary's face from her dream career goals on them as they sank down into the grave. The ground glowed white after the orbs disappeared.

"William, you will be teleported back to the day of Mary's death. This is your only chance to prevent Mary from dying of a broken heart. If you don't succeed, you will never be able to see Mary again and you will have to move on with your life without her." Gabrielle warned William.

"Don't worry Gabrielle, I won't fail this time. I'm not going to lose Mary again." William, noble about himself.

"I am very proud of you William for coming this far for your girlfriend. She's really lucky to have you in her life. Go win Mary's heart and start a life with her." Gabrielle faded.

"Thank you Gabrielle for everything and thank you for giving me a chance to be with my girl." William thanked Gabrielle.

"Your welcome Will. Now go!" Gabrielle disappeared.

The light glowed brighter as William teleported back to Wednesday, August 14th, 2015.

The white light disappeared and William found himself on Terrace Road in front of Mary.

"You should've tried harder William. I'm sorry, but I don't forgive you. After I helped you turn your life around and start fresh, but I guess I was wasting my time!" Mary turned around and walked back to her car.

"Please Mary, I beg you, I won't ever hurt you again. I promise to be completely faithful to you." William ran up to Mary's car, placed his hands on the car window, and banged on the window.

"Go away!" Mary tried to start the car.

After ten minutes of trying, Mary stopped, placed her head on the steering wheel, and broke into tears.

William stopped banging on the window, looked at his girlfriend for a couple of minutes, and left her car.

William walked back to his car heartbroken that he'll never have another chance with Mary again.

Suddenly, a car came down the hill where Mary's car blocked the intersection. A woman in the car was drunk and driving with her three friends who were also drinking.

Mary looked up and noticed the speeding car. She panicked and tried to start her car.

"Help me! Please! Someone help me!" Mary screamed and tried to get out of the car.

The next thing Mary knew was that her car door opened and William appeared.

"Come with me Mary. Take my hand, hurry!" William reached out to Mary.

"No, I can't Will. I can't trust you." Mary tried to find another way out of the car.

"Mary, you have to trust me. You need to take my hand before something bad happens."

Mary took William's hand, he helped her out of the car, and both ran to the other side of the road. They were both out of danger as the woman's car crashed into Mary's car and carried it to a tree.

"Are you all right Mare?" William checked over his girlfriend.

"I'm fine Will. Why did you save my life even though you cheated on me?"

"Mary, I am so sorry for cheating on you. I cheating for all the wrong reasons and I hurt you as a result of that. I shouldn't have never done it. If I didn't save you from your car just now, you would've been killed. I would've lost you today. If you died, I would do anything to bring back you back to life. I would go through time just to save you."

"You really mean that William. You would do anything for me if I died?"

"Of course I would do anything for you, because I love you Mary. I loved you ever since fifth grade when I first met you. Even though we've been through a lot together, I still loved you. Even though I was going out with Felicia Millerton, I still had feelings for you and I couldn't stop thinking about you. I never stopped loving you while I went out with Felicia. I've always loved you Mary... I'll never stop."

"Oh Will, you really do love me. You chose me in the end!" Mary hugged her boyfriend as fresh tears ran down her face.

"I do Mary. I rather be with you than with any other girl in this world." William held onto Mary.

"William... I forgive you, but on one condition."

"Yes honey."

"Don't ever cheat one me again."

"I promise babe, I will never break your heart again."

The paramedics and the police came to the scene as Mary and William continued to hold each other.

Meanwhile, a car pulled up to Riverside Point.

Felicia stayed in her car for a few minutes reflecting on what William said to her earlier.

"No, no, you are not the one I love! I love Mary more than you! She has been there for me when I needed help in my life while you went behind my back and cheated on me. You took advantage of me and I made a huge mistake about this test! I was so stupid for having this affair in the first place. You know, I was happy with Mary until you came back into my life! I had my life all figured out, I was about to have my family with Mary until you crashed it! Face it Felicia, I have no feelings for you and even if we did get married, I wouldn't be happy with you. You would always cheat on me! I moved on and I don't want to be with you anymore! It's over between us for good!"

"I guess William was right. It was a mistake for me to come back into his life and try to win him back. Mary does deserve him after all, she did turn his life around. Then I had to come into the picture and ruin it. Will doesn't care about his baby that I'm carrying so I'm not going to care either." Felicia touched her stomach.

"I guess I'm just a life wrecker and I don't deserve anybody or anything in my life." Felicia got out of her car.

Felicia walked over to the edge of the point that overlooked Alpine Lake. She took a small vial of cocaine, sniffed it up her nose, and threw it into the water.

"Goodbye William. I hope you are happy with your choice. My life ends here today along with your unborn child that you will never know." Felicia tearfully touched her stomach one final time.

She took a knife from her pocket and stabbed herself right in the stomach. She threw the knife into the lake and fell seventy feet into the lake below landing head first on the rocks below.

CHAPTER TWENTY-SEVEN

Happily Ever After At Last

Thursday morning, Mary woke up next to William remembering what happened yesterday.

"Mary, are you okay?" William turned over to see Mary.

"Did you save me from a car crash yesterday after I found about your affair?" Mary asked her boyfriend as he put his arms around her.

"Yes I did Mary, because I didn't want to lose you. If you died in that crash yesterday... I would be nothing without you."

"Just like you said, that affair was meaningless and you chose me. I'm very proud of you for all the accomplishments you made so far in your life." Mary hugged her boyfriend.

"I'm never going back to my old ways. I'm going to stay my committed self to you and be a police officer."

"That's all I needed to hear. I'm going to jump in the shower real quick. I'll see you in a couple of minutes." Mary kissed William, got out of bed, and headed for the bathroom.

"I'll start making breakfast for us." Will got out of bed.

"Sounds good. I miss you already." Mary ached for William.

"I miss you too. I'll see you in the kitchen." William walked out of the room.

William grabbed the newspaper outside the apartment door as the pancakes cooked. He looked through the paper to find Felicia's face on the back of the front page.

The article stated that Felicia Millerton was found near Alpine Park Pier. She had cocaine in her system for the last couple of weeks, there was no baby, and the Coroner ruled out her death as a suicide.

"Felicia used me all along especially when she told me that she was pregnant! She wasn't pregnant in the first place. I'm just glad that she is finally gone out of my life!"

William ignored the article and flipped over to the other side to find an advertisement for his girlfriend's book.

"Things are going back to normal for me and Mary. All I need to do is propose to her." William got up and walked over to the stove.

Mary came out of the bathroom soon afterwards.

"How's it going there chef?" Mary stood next to Will.

"I'm almost done cooking sweetheart. Oh, take a look at the newspaper. There's an advertisement for your Star sisters book." William brought two plates of food to the table.

"Really oh my god, I hope I will receives great reviews for the book." Mary looked at the paper.

"You will, don't give up. Like you always told me, keep going at your dreams." William knelt next to Mary and took her hand.

"You're right. I'm not going to give up with you at my side." Mary hugged William happily.

Saturday, August 17th, 2015 was Mary's birthday. William waited for Mary to come home from Kaylin and Eric's apartment.

There was a small cake in the middle of the table in the dim-lit kitchen.

"Okay everything is all set. I got the ring in my pocket and Mary should be home any minute. This is it, I'm finally proposing to my girlfriend and settle down with her. I'm not going to mess this up this time. It's going to go perfectly and no one is going to stop me from proposing to Mary!" William felt the ring in his pocket.

Suddenly, Will heard the door open and heard,

"I'm home!" Mary called to William.

Will snuck into the dining room leading into the living room.

"Why are the lights turned off? William, are you here?" Mary walked towards the kitchen.

Will turned on the lights and Mary discovered the cake in the candle lit kitchen.

"Happy birthday honey." William wrapped his arms around Mary's waist.

"Oh sweetie, you didn't have to do this for me." Mary, with a surprised look.

"Well, I wanted to make it up to you after the last few days that happened between us. I'm never going to be that same guy that I was last week. I took my test and I chose you in the end. That's why I wanted to ask you something that I've been trying to say since we graduated college."

"What did you wanted to tell me?"

"Mary, I know that we've been through a lot throughout the years. I know I've done a lot of stupid things in the past to you, but I figured it out that it's you that I should be with and I want to keep it like that. I love you so much Mary Radcliffe and I want to spend the rest of my life with you. Will you marry me Mary Radcliffe?" William got down on one knee and proposed to Mary.

"Yes, I will marry you William!" Mary accepted William's proposal.

"Mary, thank you so much. I promise that I will be the best husband to you and I'll make everything count in our marriage." William put the ring on her finger.

"You will be a great husband to me. Don't have any worries. You have been the greatest boyfriend to me ever since we got back together in the summer of 2007. Nothing can come between our relationship now that we are taking the big step now. I am ready to be committed to you and only you." Mary wrapped her arms around Will.

"Then we are getting married!" William swung his girl and kissed her.

Months past, Mary's book became a huge success around the nation. William got a full-time job at the police station after he got his police certification. They planned out their wedding throughout the fall and the date was scheduled for Saturday, May 7th, 2016.

"I can't believe that I'm finally getting married to William. This is the most happiest day of my life!" Mary looked at the mirror as Kaylin and Natalie helped her get ready.

"Mary, I am so happy for you. I'm glad you stayed with William." Natalie happily to her friend.

"Well at least Felicia got what she deserved in the end. She almost broke you and William apart! At least Will came to his senses and chose you in the end."

"Kaylin, I don't want to talk about Felicia on my big day okay."

"Sorry Mary."

"Mary, it's time. We're ready for you." Susan walked into the room.

"Okay. Here is goes." Mary smiled and walked out of the room with her bouquet of pink roses.

In the church room, music played, everyone was in their seats, and William waited for the ceremony to start. William wore a black suit with a silver-white dress shirt and tie. As soon as the doors opened, the music changed. Once Natalie and Kaylin walked down the aisle, Mary appeared with Andrew.

William watched Mary come down the aisle with her father in a white long sparkling dress. Her hair in a bun, her make up perfect, and beautiful.

The music stopped and everyone sat down.

"Who gives this woman to this man?"

"I do along with her mother." Andrew said as Petra got up and stood next to Mary.

Mary took her father's hand and Andrew gave her to William. William took Mary's hand and walked over to Father Peter.

"We are gathered here today to celebrate the union of this man and this woman. They have come a long way down the road of commitment and they are ready to be unified in holy matrimony. Do you William Ryan Valmont take Mary Petra Radcliffe to be your wife?"

"I do take Mary Petra Radcliffe to be my wife." William received the ring from Ron and placed it onto Mary's finger.

"Do you Mary Petra Radcliffe take William Ryan Valmont to be your husband?"

"I do take William Ryan Valmont to be my husband." Mary received the ring from Natalie and placed it onto Will's finger.

"I here by proclaim William and Mary, husband and wife. You may kiss the bride." Father Peter concluded the ceremony.

William kissed Mary slowly and passionately for their first kiss as husband and wife while everyone clapped and cheered for them.

The wedding reception took place at Langston Park in the pavilion.

"Ladies and gentlemen, I would like to present you, Mr. and Mrs. Valmont! Let's start off the celebration with their first dance together as husband and wife!" Eric announced to everyone as William and Mary entered the pavilion.

"I can't believe that we are finally married at last!"

"I'm happy that you are happy darling. I promise that I will be a wonderful husband to you and our family." William danced with Mary.

"You are already a wonderful husband to me. You just need to love me and take care of me for the rest of my life. That's all you need to do." Mary swayed to the music and touched William's face.

"I will love you forever Mary. You don't need to worry." William looked at his bride and stroked her hair.

The two laughed soon afterwards.

"I love you Mary Valmont." William's nose touched Mary's nose.

"I love you too William Valmont." Mary looked deeply into Will's eyes.

William kissed Mary deeply as they continued to dance throughout the night.

Fate brought these two lovers together and broke them apart, but after going through five missions and collecting spheres, William Valmont won Mary Radcliffe and brought her back to life. Now they can live and start their new lives together.

William got his wish in the end and learned his lesson on hurting the ones he loves.

Good things can happen if you believe in yourself, miracles, and love.

THE END